He married me for a mile of road!

Tears stung Mary's eyes as she stared at the documents Bruce's lawyer had laid before her. For my land, she thought bitterly, and he's sitting in there expecting me to sign it all away. We'll adopt Becky and he'll have me in his bed every night for the fun of it. Until the road gets built.

And then what? He's already bought me, with ten percent of his rotten stock. And I promised to love, honor and cherish him! And I promised to obey him!

She picked up the pen and with large, wild strokes she wrote *"No!"* across the signature line.

Then she walked trembling out of Bruce Latimore's office, leaving behind her shattered dreams.

Books by Emma Goldrick

HARLEQUIN ROMANCES
2661—THE ROAD

HARLEQUIN PRESENTS
688—AND BLOW YOUR HOUSE DOWN

These books may be available at your local bookseller.

For a list of all titles currently available,
send your name and address to:

Harlequin Reader Service
P.O. Box 52040, Phoenix, AZ 85072-2040
Canadian address: P.O. Box 2800, Postal Station A,
5170 Yonge St., Willowdale, Ont. M2N 5T5

The Road

Emma Goldrick

Harlequin Books

TORONTO • NEW YORK • LONDON
AMSTERDAM • PARIS • SYDNEY • HAMBURG
STOCKHOLM • ATHENS • TOKYO • MILAN

Original hardcover edition published in 1984
by Mills & Boon Limited

ISBN 0-373-02661-7

Harlequin Romance first edition December 1984

CHAPTER ONE

FROM one thousand feet up he could see the road clearly as the helicopter swung them in a great arc south of Boston. My road, he exulted. One hundred and seventy miles of road—no, damn it—one hundred and sixty-nine miles of road. 'But I've got that witch this time!'

'Are we going to see a witch?' The child at his knee shrieked in glee. 'A real witch?'

'Yes, a real old witch,' he laughed in return. But as he looked out the window his glee turned to disgust. One hundred and sixty-nine miles of road, stretching in a great eight-lane circle around Boston, from the New Hampshire border to the shore at Cape Cod. Except for the one mile directly below them, where the highway lay in two parts, separated by an open mile of farm land, speckled with Jersey cows, green-tasselled corn, and gradually yellowing hay. One damn mile! But I've got her this time! He patted the briefcase which bulged with the report.

'I never did see no witch,' the child repeated excitedly.

'Well, you'll see one today,' he laughed. 'And we've got her right by the tail this time, baby!'

'A witch with a tail!' The child bounced up and down in her seat. He eyed her with a pleasure he had never felt before. She's six years old, he told himself. Six years old, and I hardly know her. And look how she's dressed: dungaree overalls, a pull-over red shirt, and her blonde hair cut close to her head. 'To avoid the summer heat,' Mrs Driscoll kept telling him. There was something wrong with the whole picture. For five years

he had travelled the world, building up his construction
company, while Mattie grew up in the Driscoll
household. The kid needs something, she's too formal,
too stiff. That's the first time I've heard her laugh since
I came home!

The helicopter banked to the left, drawing his
attention back to the window. To his surprise they were
making an approach to a cleared meadow on the farm
itself, instead of at the roadhead, where a car waited for
them. He moved to correct the pilot and then stopped.
They circled the old clapboard farmhouse; white, of
course, what other colour would you find on a New
England farmhouse? There was a pebbled walkway that
led down the hill from the house and out to the rural
road. Half-way down the path was an immense tree
stump worn smooth by age and weather, still showing
the decayed centre that must have caused the tree to
fall, and sitting on the stump was a woman, head back,
hand to her forehead to shield her eyes from the bright
August sun as she followed the flight of the helicopter.
She was a gay spot of colour against the dark brown of
the stump. A brilliant white blouse, demurely buttoned,
and a swirling cranberry dirndl skirt. Then the
helicopter turned again, scattering dust and grass-ends
into the air before it settled on the meadow.

He slid the big door sideways, jumped down to the
ground, and turned to lift up his arms. The little girl
smiled down at him and jumped. He swung her down to
the ground as the pilot cut the engines and the big blades
began to slow down. With one hand in Mattie's and the
other on the briefcase, he ducked his head and moved
quickly out from under the cone of the helicopter blades.
The big machine coughed twice, then fell silent

Mattie pulled him to a stop while she stared in awe at
the still-moving blades. The country sounds were
gradually returning, as if they had all been frightened
off by the noise of the big machine.

'You've certainly come in style this time, Mr Francis!' The voice behind him was a cool, soft contralto, with husky overtones. He turned around, tugging Mattie away from her fascination with the aircraft, 'Oh! I'm sorry. You're not—where's Mr Francis?'

'Mr Francis is in the hospital with a bleeding ulcer,' he said sternly, it would be good to put a little scare into this little thing before they talked. She could hardly be more than five foot four, her light brown hair bound in two braids down the sides of her head, and looped forward over both shoulders. Grey eyes? Green, perhaps. A pert, heart-shaped face, cheeks tanned and a freckled nose without a trace of make-up. Bare legs, with sandals on her feet, and a magnificent figure, not entirely hidden by the loose blouse or the swinging skirt. Not beautiful, but——? How old? Twenty, or maybe twenty-five? Must have been a real child bride!

'I'm Latimore. Bruce Latimore.' He pushed forward one massive hand, she tendered her tiny one, and giggled as it disappeared into his.

'Mrs Chase,' she responded, 'Mary Chase. Mr Francis is ill? How terrible!' Her voice was filled with honest concern as she gestured him up the hill towards the house. 'I've dealt with Mr Francis for almost three years now. And his wife? How are the chidren taking all this?'

'You seem to be very familiar with Mr Francis,' he commented coldly. So that's what's been going on, a little hanky-panky on the side, to keep that fool Francis sweet!

'Well, yes of course I am,' she retorted, smoothing down her skirt to repress the spurt of anger which came over her. 'He's a fine man, well thought of in these parts, you must have worked him to the bone to give him a case of ulcers!' She flipped her braids at him indignantly, and started up the hill.

'For your information, Mrs Chase,' he said as he

started out after her, 'you are the only job Mr Francis
has had for the past two years. Just you!'

'Just me?' she asked softly, swinging around towards
him. They had come back to the huge stump beside the
path. She fingered the top of it while she contemplated
him. 'Just me?' she repeated. 'Look at this, Mr
Latimore,' she patted the old stump, 'it was two
hundred and twenty-five years old when lightning struck
it. When it was young it was the Liberty Tree for
Eastboro—you know about Liberty Trees? No, I didn't
think you did. And now look down there,' she gestured
down the hill to where the stone ruins of a clump of old
houses barely topped the unmown grass, 'the town used
to be there,' she continued, 'until they built the Post
Road. And then everyone moved down there around
the bend. About 1795, that was. This is a place steeped
in tradition, Mr Latimore, have you ever considered
that?'

He waved his hand in a half-hearted gesture of
protest. 'My family didn't come over here until 1919,'
he said. 'I don't make the world, Mrs Chase, only this
one little road.' During all this conversation Mattie had
been hiding behind her father's leg, still clutching his
hand. Now she came out of her shelter and stared at the
woman before her. 'You don't look like no witch,' she
said in that puzzled frank tone that children seem
naturally to use when embarrassing their elders. Her
father shook her little hand in warning.

'Oho,' Mary Chase said, 'so that's the problem! Your
father told you I was a witch?' She stooped down to the
little child, brushing her skirts down around her as she
settled 'You are a—handsome boy? What lovely long
eyelashes!'

'I ain't no boy,' Mattie pouted at her. 'I ain't.'

'Why of course not,' Mary responded. 'I can see that
now. You're a girl! How lucky you are!'

'You hear that, Daddy,' Mattie shrilled to her father.

And then she turned back to Mary. 'How come I'm lucky?' she asked wistfully.

'How come? Lots of reasons. It's a big advantage to be a girl, didn't you know that?'

'No, I din't know that. All the Driscolls are boys, and they're bigger than me, and say nasty things, and beat up on me when nobody's looking!'

'Well, doesn't that prove it? They're jealous! Just look at us, we're both prettier than your daddy, aren't we?'

'Why—so we are. Both of us?' The little voice sounded extremely doubtful about the whole affair.

'Both of us are. And we don't have to shave every day as your daddy does, would you like to have whiskers?'

'Oh no, they scratch. My mother was a girl.'

'There, that proves it. Being a mother is the best job in the world, and only girls can be mothers. Come on, let's go up to the house and have some cookies and milk. Would you like that?'

'Oh my yes. Can Daddy come too?'

'If he wants to.'

My God, he told himself as he followed the two of them up the path to the house. Five minutes and she's taken control; not only of the conversation, but I'll be damned if she hasn't stolen my daughter to boot! Smooth. And I thought she was a country kid! I need a night's sleep, I shouldn't have come directly from the Venezuela trip to this one, and I shouldn't have brought Mattie with me. Two strikes already. Whatever happened to the big tycoon?

The two ahead of him were chattering away like a pair of magpies. His daughter was skipping, while holding the woman's hand, and laughing at the top of her lungs. He glared at the woman's back, not fully understanding what it was that was gnawing at him; lovely hips, well rounded; beautiful legs; a straight

strong back; and those idiotic braids, now swinging
down her back almost to her waist. And Mattie; she
had changed since they climbed out of the helicopter:
how? Think man, think!

The two ahead of him mounted the steps to the
broad verandah that encircled the house, and as they
did so the front door opened, and a young girl came
out.

'Becky!' the woman called. 'We've visitors. Put the
kettle on please.'

'Yeah, Ma. Right away.' The girl at the door turned
back into the house. They followed her in. His
calculations were upset again; the girl in the doorway
was certainly fourteen or fifteen. *Yeah Ma*. Dark,
raven-winged hair, curling up against her scalp, dark
black eyes, darker skin, compared to her—mother? And
whatever her age, she already stood a good three inches
taller than her—mother? That must make Mary Chase
thirty-five? Forty? Impossible, damn it, take away the
kids, and she'd be eighteen! He tried to shake the
cobwebs out of his head as he took the proffered seat in
the old-fashioned sitting room.

Mary watched him. It was her favourite occupation,
watching people and assessing them. He had been
prepared to give her the autocratic male approach until
she had diverted the conversation to the beautiful little
girl, and now Becky had given him another jolt. Well,
she told herself, he'll have one or two more jolts before
the day is over! She looked around her crowded living
room with the pleasure of remembrance. There were no
antiques, it was all Grand Rapids, 1893, built solidly
and comfortably. Massive legs on massive chairs to
hold massive men. Like her husband, the Colonel.
Funny, even now, five years after he died, she still
thought of him as the Colonel. He had been a big
man—as big as this one, sitting back in the Colonel's
favourite chair. 'Will you have coffee, Mr Latimore,'

she asked him. 'Mattie, would you like to go out to the kitchen and help Becky?' The little girl bounced off the couch and followed Mary's pointing finger.

'She's a lovely child, Mr Latimore,' she added as the little girl raced out the door.

'Would you mind calling me Bruce? All my friends call me Bruce,' he asked.

'Do they indeed,' she said quietly.

'You have a lovely—daughter—too,' he prodded.

'Rebecca? Yes, she is lovely. She's almost a carbon copy of her father. He was a tall man, dark haired. She's fifteen now. A lovely fifteen. The Colonel would be very proud of her, if he could know.'

'The Colonel?'

'My husband. His name was Henry, but we called him the Colonel. He was a retired officer from the regular army, you know.'

'No, I didn't know, I thought he was a farmer.'

'Well, that too. He bought this farm when he retired from the army. And he made a successful experimental farm out of it. You like our place?'

'Yes, it's very nice,' he monotoned. 'But perhaps we could get down to business, er—Mrs Chase?'

'Of course, if you like,' she returned. 'Although the coffee is here now, should we try the refreshments before the business?'

Becky bustled back into the room, pushing a trolley in front of her. Mattie followed, carrying four mugs. Mary guided the lot to the low coffee table in front of the couch and poured coffee for herself and Latimore. Becky declined, and received a cup of milk. Mattie, imitating Becky at every turn, took milk too. The little girl had a puzzled look on her face.

'Becky says she's not old, Daddy,' she said as she broke into the conversation. 'And they don't got no brooms. Not that kind, anyway. Becky says they only got an electric broom, and nobody could ride on that, cause the plug would fall out of the socket. So I don't think she can be no old witch.'

'No,' Becky joined in, struggling to keep a straight face, 'I give you my solemn assurance that Ma is not an old witch. In fact, she's only twenty-one.'

He was shaken by the subtle attack from two sides at the same time. 'Maybe we'd better talk about that privately,' he hurried to say, trying to cut off his daughter's further discussion. 'I apologise for that, Mrs Chase,' he muttered. His face was turning the colour of a boiled lobster. 'We were speculating—in the helicopter, you know—and I guess you know all about little ears?'

'About little ears? Yes, I know all about them,' she replied. 'And I'm not insulted, Mr—er—Latimore. Most modern women have a little of the witch about them, you know.'

'Well, if that doesn't insult you,' he chuckled, fingering the knot of his tie, 'perhaps you wouldn't mind answering the other question that keeps popping up. You're twenty-one?'

'A family joke,' she assured him. 'I swore that I would never go past my twenty-first birthday.'

'But we've celebrated a lot more than one of your twenty-first birthdays, Ma,' Becky broke in.

'Now missy, mind your manners,' Mary said quietly. The girl's laugh broke off instantly. She squared herself around in the chair and brushed down her yellow cotton skirt. 'Yes ma'am,' she answered. There was an uneasy silence, which Mattie broke up.

'And she doesn't have no tail, either, Daddy,' she pronounced. 'So how could we catch her by the tail? I think you got it all wrong.'

'Yes, I guess I have, pet,' he sighed. 'These cookies are good, Mrs Chase. A store product?'

'Not in this house,' Becky commented. 'Ma bakes them all herself. And the bread, and biscuits, and, oh lordy, Ma can do anything!'

'The original Superwoman,' Mary laughed. 'You mustn't get too carried away by Becky's talk, Mr Latimore. I do what any farm woman does. I've had considerable practice. Now Becky, why don't you take Mattie out to the fields. I have a notion she may not be too closely connected with cows and pigs and chickens and things.'

He watched them closely as Becky immediately took the young girl's hand and led her out of the room. 'Remarkable,' he said, 'and not a quiver or an objection.'

'You mean Becky?' She had slipped off her sandals and now coiled her feet up underneath her. 'It's not all my doing. The Colonel was a strict disciplinarian. And I've just carried on in his footsteps, so to speak. Becky is a nice adult person, someone I can talk to intelligently, someone who cares when I ache. And she has her own goals. We go along very well together.'

'Unusual,' he said as he unzipped his briefcase. 'But now——'

'Before we get down to business,' she interrupted, 'may I ask *you* a personal question?' He stopped what he was doing, looked over at her expectantly, and nodded.

'Why is it that your daughter doesn't know she's a girl?'

The question stunned him. It was not the subject he had expected, and it made him stop and think. Was that the thing he had been groping for, up there in the helicopter. Why doesn't my daughter know she's a girl? Who's fault is that?

'I—I don't follow you,' he stammered. 'She—of course she knows that she's not a boy. Is that what you mean?'

'No, that's not what I mean, Mr Latimore.' Mary leaned over the coffee table towards him to emphasise what she was saying. 'She doesn't *know* she's a girl. The positive things; all the little secret things that girls know, and boys never find out. Why doesn't she know them?'

'I don't really know what you mean,' he answered defensively. 'Her mother died when Mattie was one year old. I have to be away a great deal of the time. Mattie stays with a family—a highly recommended family—and—oh hell, I don't know, do I. She needs a mother!'

'I guess you're right,' Mary said. She leaned back in her seat, nursing the last chocolate chip cookie from the plate.

'You wouldn't perhaps be looking for such a job?' he asked harshly, and now she could see the glint of steel in the back of his eyes, the predatory poise of the hawk.

'No, I don't think so,' she answered quietly. 'I do seem to have my fingers in too many pies already.'

She would have sworn that he muttered 'you'd better believe it' under his breath, but she had thrown enough barbs for one day. She smiled sweetly at him, and let it pass.

'Now, here's the document we've been waiting for,' he said as he drew out a manuscript, almost five hundred pages long from his briefcase. 'An Environmental Impact Study for Highway I 695 (proposed).'

'It certainly seems big enough,' she said, in some awe. 'Is that what took you nine months to prepare?' He passed it over to her. It was so heavy that she almost dropped it on to the dishes on the coffee table.

'Yes, it is,' he almost snarled, and then remembered his manners. 'If you'll remember, the Superior Court ordered all construction halted because there was no report on the taking by eminent domain of Somerfield farms. And of course, your having my surveyors arrested for trespass didn't help a great deal either. So here it is. According to the direction of the judge, your lawyer has one copy, two have been submitted to the court for study, and arguments will be heard the day after tomorrow. I don't suppose you'd be interested in the details, of course. I expect we'll have the bulldozers start to work next Monday.'

Of course, she thought, what a thorough chauvinist. Of course, female, you wouldn't be able to understand the details! 'I thought you might have planned early action,' she chuckled. 'Your heavy equipment was moved in at six o'clock this morning. Very disturbing, you know. You will give us notice before you start to knock down the house?' She gave the appearance of idly thumbing through the thick report, when in reality her quick eye was scanning the Table of Contents. He settled back in his chair, and was lighting up a cheroot, a very wide and satisfied smile on his face.

'Of course we will,' he replied. He plays his voice like an actor, she noted. Emphasis, change of tones, pauses—the works—it's almost as good as an organ recital. She struggled hard to repress the giggles. He was fumbling around a little self-consciously. For a— whatever you are, Mary thought, you're a little lost in the country, aren't you love!

'I don't think—I don't seem to be able to find an ash-tray,' he apologised. The room was getting too hot for him, for some reason, he struggled to release the knot of his tie, holding his cigar as if it had suddenly become a rattle-snake.

'No. We never use them,' she answered blandly. 'None of us smoke, and we try to discourage others from doing so.'

She left him to fumble for a minute or two longer, but when it looked as if he were about to stub out the cigar on the palm of his hand she reached him over a saucer, then turned back to the document, turning pages slowly, looking for a specific item. When she looked up again the cigar had disappeared, although there seemed to be a faint trail of smoke coming from his jacket pocket.

'And you've sent a copy to my lawyer?' she queried.

'Mr Momson. Yes, we have. Funny old fellow, that one.'

'Funny? If you mean curious, I'd agree.' She continued her thumbing through the report, but her mind was guarding her tongue. 'After all, Mr Momson is eighty-two years old.'

'I really don't understand him,' he sighed. 'I've examined the record. Momson looks as if he couldn't get a client off from a parking ticket, and yet he's opposed us with some of the most legalistic arguments I've ever read.'

'He doesn't have a lot of energy,' she proposed. 'But then again you realise that I'm the only client he has. He retired about ten years ago, and only agreed to help me because he was one of the Colonel's closest friends.'

'The Colonel—oh yes, your husband.'

'Yes,' she sighed. 'I miss him. We were only married a short time, but I miss him. You're lucky, Mr Latimore. If the Colonel were here he'd have met your bulldozers with a battery of 105 Howitzers. He was a man of singularly—short—temper. I guess that's the polite way of saying it.'

'Ruled his roost with an iron hand, did he? You too?'

'Oh yes,' she laughed, wiping her eye. 'Yes indeed. We all had our place defined in the pecking order. Although from time to time I had the feeling that his dog Rover outranked me. Love, honour, and obey, it was——' and now she was unable to hold back the tears. He leaned over the table and handed her his large handkerchief. She managed to dry her tears, thinking 'oh aren't you the well-trained diplomat'!

'It's not unusual,' she told him. 'Crying, that is. I'm a very emotional female. I'm sure you know the type. Yes, it was love, honour, and obey with the Colonel, and I loved every minute of it. Every minute.'

'I envy him,' he said. She looked up quickly, but could read nothing but sincerity in his eyes. 'Thank you,' she replied.

She closed the report and set it back on the table. 'It seems so—large,' she chuckled. 'And surely you don't expect me to understand it all?'

'Of course not,' he laughed in return. 'It's written in legal jargon, for the judge, but you can take my word for it, it's thorough, and it's complete.'

Look at that self-satisfied look, she thought. She settled back in her seat and really looked at him for the first time. Five foot eleven, perhaps six foot? Built bulky. Not fat. There's not an ounce of fat showing. Moves well. Plenty of coordination. A square sort of face. It comes straight down the sides to a square jaw. A big firm mouth. When he smiles it almost covers his face. A Roman nose—it looks as if somebody had stepped on it at one time or another. Deep-set dark eyes, with heavy eyebrows overshadowing them. Predatory, that's the key word. I wonder what he does for the State, or for the Latimore Construction Corporation? Holy Toledo, the Latimore Construction Company! He must be one of the poor relatives. But not hardly. He acts like one of the Conquistadores, not like one of the peons.

'I suppose I must take your word for that.' She smiled back at him, trying to conceal the little trill of excitement that ran down her spine. 'You have looked at the alternatives?' she prodded.

'Alternatives? I suppose not,' he returned. I haven't paid this job a great deal of attention. Until Mr Francis reported in to the hospital, I guess all I've done is read quarterly status reports. But there's hardly any need, is there. When the court says "go" it should take us about four weeks to link up the two sections of the road.'

'And ruin one of the finest experimental farms in all of New England.'

'I wasn't aware of that,' he said softly. 'But the road is for the common good, you know. That's why the law gives the right to take by eminent domain. Just what is your problem?'

'Oh nothing, really,' she told him. 'Your road is going right through the middle of our farm, taking the best bottom land we have, and separating the two parts of what's left so we would have to drive six miles to cross to the other side. And I'm afraid the noise level would drive our cows mad. Now look here.' She pulled out one of the ever-ready county maps, and indicated another line to him. 'If you would swing your road south, a matter of about a mile, you could take all this rocky land on the south perimeter of our farm and leave us a usable piece of land. It would be a nice compromise.'

'Yes, well, I'm sorry, Mrs Chase, but it's too late for that, I'm afraid. The state is committed to this straight road, and we have to follow the political dictates, you know.'

I'll just bet you do, she told herself. You and all your friends in the legislature. The best legislature that money can buy. Everybody gets a piece of the action. And if your own grandmother owned this farm you'd do exactly the same, wouldn't you! She folded her arms across her ample bosom and glared at him. Just you wait, she threatened silently. You just wait. You're going to get yours, Mr Big Shot! She was almost prepared to tell him about it when Becky and Mattie burst into the room, filling it with sunshine chatter.

'Gee Daddy,' Mattie said as she danced up to him and seized both his hands. 'The chickens are running like mad, and the cows were all lying down chewing their dinner, and there was this goat with a bell on, and——'

'Whoa up, princess,' he laughed. He gathered her up in his arms and gave her a hug and a kiss. 'We have to be getting back to Boston, baby. I've finished my business with Mrs Chase, and I suppose they want to get on with the farm work.'

'Do you really have to be going so soon?' Mary unfolded from her position, stretched to find her sandals, and looked at him enquiringly. 'Mr Francis always stayed for supper.'

'No, not today,' he replied. 'We do have to get back. I'm dining out tonight, and we have to get Mathilda back to the Driscolls.'

'No, Daddy!' The little girl stamped her foot. There were tears in her eyes. 'You said you were going to stay with me, Daddy!'

'I did, pumpkin,' he soothed. 'But I forgot I had a dinner date with Miss Hawkins. You liked Miss Hawkins.'

'No I don't, not any more,' the little girl bawled. 'I like it here. I want to stay with Becky and Mrs Chase.'

There were noises in the kitchen behind them, loud enough to distract them all. Mary smiled. Lucky man, she thought. Off-stage noises distract child from temper tantrum. Serves you right! The kitchen door opened halfway.

'Hey Ma,' the deep male voice from the kitchen reverberated around the room. 'Anna wants that recipe thing for your special clam chowder.'

'It's in the recipe box,' she called back, 'the little box marked Addresses. Come through for a minute, Henry.'

The door opened fully. The man who came through was a tall dark-haired farmer, apparently about thirty years old, wearing worn denims and a dusty short-sleeved shirt.

'Mr Latimore,' she said, 'may I present my son Henry. Henry, this gentleman is from the road company.' And try that on for size she whispered under her breath. She could almost see his eyeballs rattle as he tried to compute *her* age based on the new evidence.

The two men shook hands somewhat reluctantly. Henry was too plain spoken to play the game that she and Becky enjoyed, for the moment he kept silent.

'Henry is actually the farmer of the family,' she explained to Latimore in her quiet contralto. 'He and his very new wife live in the other house down the way from us. And this is Mattie, Mr Latimore's daughter.'

The introduction brought a big smile to Henry's face. He loved children above everything else in the world, except Anna. 'Hi Mattie,' he called. 'Nice to have you come see us. Oh Ma, those darn varmints were back in among the chickens again. I'm going to have to trap them.'

'I wanna stay at your house,' Mattie said solemnly.

'But you can't. We're leaving now,' her father commanded her. 'Glad to have met you Henry, Becky. Mrs Chase, I suppose we won't be meeting again. I did enjoy it all.' He turned towards the door, dragging a reluctant Mattie with him. Mary walked them to the door, and stood in the open doorway watching as they hurried down the hill to the waiting helicopter.

'They won't be back again?' Henry was standing just behind her when he asked. There was a touch of anxiety in his voice.

'Oh, they'll be back,' Mary laughed. 'Probably Friday or Saturday, I would say. This one is a driver. And poor Mr Francis is in the hospital. Isn't that awful?'

'Come on, Ma,' he laughed. He dropped one muscular arm across her small shoulders. 'If it were me, I would sooner farm the Sahara Desert than to tangle with you. Is that why you were playing the Wicked Stepmother routine?'

She turned around, laughing up at both of them, sharing their secret happily. 'I don't do it for wickedness,' she told them. 'The Colonel wanted you both to own the farm, and I promised him I would see it happen. And I will. Now you, Becky, go and telephone Mr Momson. He said he'd wait late in his office. Tell him that the Environmental Impact statement makes no mention of the wetlands. He'll know what I mean. The new State law on wetlands prohibits all construction that will disturb the balance of the swamp ecology. And you, Henry, did you do what I asked you to?'

'Yes, I sure did,' he replied. 'I cleared a roadway into the west boundary. And sure enough, there were some Indian artifacts, just as you said. You know, I'm beginning to enjoy this!'

'Don't count your chickens,' she sighed as she took each of them by the arm. 'This one means to get his road built, come hell or high water. I don't think there's a single thing he wouldn't do to get his road connected. But that poor little girl! Did she talk to you at all, Becky?'

'Only a little bit, Ma. She's lonesome. She loves her father, but he's hardly ever home, poor kid. She's just the way I would have been if the Colonel hadn't married you. What a lucky day that was for us, wasn't it Henry?'

'Lucky is right.' Henry gathered his tiny stepmother up in his arms and hugged her gently. 'Lucky is right,' he repeated.

'Well, I was lucky too,' she said quietly. 'You will never know how much it means to me to have been married to your father.'

She moved to the centre of the living room and started to collect the dirty dishes, her mind deep in the past. Becky immediately shouldered her aside and took over the task. Mary watched as the raven hair swung around her shoulders, her adolescent figure trim in her white blouse and blue jeans. Fifteen years; Mary counted the litany of her days in the old house. It had been fifteen years ago, just two days after Becky was born, that Mary Kate and her mother had come to the farmhouse on the hill. Had come to keep house for the Colonel while the first Mrs Chase had slid down that deep depression that eventually led to her death from birth trauma. Mary Kate had been a boisterous twelve then. And four years later Mary's mother had died, stricken abruptly by a massive stroke, without warning so that one minute she had been laughing and the next she was gone. Sixteen-year-old Mary Kate had drawn close to four-year-old Becky in that dark time, and it seemed pre-ordained that Mary Kate would take over the running of the house. A short year later she had married the Colonel. A seventeen-year-old bride, safe and secure in the hands of a man who knew the world's worth, and respected honesty. And then, five years after the marriage, the Colonel himself had been struck down, but not before he required a promise of her. And now, at twenty-seven, it was a promise she meant to keep.

'But your Mr Latimore,' Becky interrupted her chain of thought, 'he's certainly a tasty man!'

Mary stood back out of the way of busy hands. 'Tasty? I don't know about that—and he's not *my* Mr Latimore. But you know something? He has a lot of your father's dominant force in him. And I somehow got the feeling that he's the sort of man who would have a lot of love to give, if he ever got his priorities right.'

'Ma! At your age! What *are* you thinking of?' Becky giggled. Mary dropped back into the overstuffed chair, blushing, to think it all over.

CHAPTER TWO

As it happened, he did not show up on Friday as she had expected, but there were too many other problems around to keep her busy. On Thursday she baked all day, making her special crunch-crust bread for the bake sale at the Congregational Church in the village. She had saved two loaves, just in case, but a late-afternoon emergency call from the Pastor had been enough for her to send Becky down on her bicycle with the remaining loaves. Friday she spent the morning going over her notes and the afternoon on house cleaning. Then, as usual on Tuesdays and Fridays, she was off to Boston to school.

When she got back that night, tired and a little cross from the idiocies of the lecturer, she was surprised to see that the lights were still on. Becky was waiting up for her, tired and excited. They shared hot chocolate while the girl told her all the details of the square-dance to which her brother and his wife had taken her. They both showered and went off to their separate rooms. But she knew that something was bothering Becky, so she forced herself to stay awake, patiently. Sure enough, just a few minutes before twelve there was a knock on her open door, and the girl came in, dressed in her shortie night gown.

'Ma?' she said hesitantly from the shadow of the door. Mary flicked on her bed lamp and patted the area on the big double bed beside her. The girl hurried over and climbed in beside her.

After a pause, while Becky settled herself, Mary said, 'Tell me about the something special that happened to you tonight.'

Becky giggled at her. 'You really are a witch, aren't you!'

'Did you ever doubt it? What happened?'

'Ma, I met—there was this boy.'

'Aha! The story of every girl's life,' she teased, 'there was this boy. Does he have a name?'

'Harold, Ma. Doctor Everett's son Harold. He's—nice. We danced four sets, and then we walked out for a few minutes. It was hot, you know.'

'I know, dear,' she chuckled. 'Go ahead.'

Becky leaned her head on her stepmother's shoulder and began a long meandering recital that told all about her first 'real' kiss, her first real emotion. Mary listened. She was a good listener, even the Colonel had said that. And when the story was fully told, and some passages twice repeated, she cleared her throat.

'You're not mad at me, Ma?'

'Mad at you? Nonsense. You haven't made any terrible mistakes, but I have. That *Sex Education* course at the school, Becky. I thought it took care of everything. So now you listen to your mama while we have another lecture. First of all, it's perfectly normal for a girl your age to react to the male. Perfectly normal. God devised the sex game to insure the survival of the race. That's why it's more fun than any other game in the world—providing both players know the rules!'

And then quietly, but with unmistakable enthusiasm she explained to her daughter all the intimate details of how the game is played, what effect it had on female emotions, and what the rules were. Which took them until two in the morning, two additional cups of hot chocolate, and more than a dozen repetitions of 'No! You didn't, Ma!' before Becky finally closed her eyes for just a moment to think of another question, and fell fast asleep.

Mary watched as she slept, her lips slightly parted,

and her long, loose, black hair sprayed out over the pillow like silk filaments. Then she pulled up the light coverlet over them both, slid down in the bed, said a prayer of thanks, and followed Becky down the dream-path. But where Becky was smiling, undoubtedly because of Harold, Mary herself, for some reason she was unable to assess, was finding Bruce Latimore's face popping up in *her* dreams.

The next morning was Saturday, a sleep-in day, but Mary was awakened by the uproar of engines at seven o'clock. She groaned her way out of bed, brushed aside the white and gold curtains at her bedroom window, and peered out. Five huge transports had arrived down by the bend in the road, and were loading up the earth-mover and the four bulldozers that had stood there, like an enemy armoured column for the past week. By eight-thirty the transports were loaded and they roared up the incomplete segment of I-695 and out of sight.

Becky was still asleep, huddled up on her stomach, with the second pillow over her head. Mary sighed for her own lost youth, took down her old cotton robe, and went downstairs for breakfast. Her books were still cluttering up the kitchen table where she had dropped them last night. She picked up the heaviest of them and sneered at it. Torts, by C. Shreber. Who was, of course, her own professor. She was caught in the University merry-go-round, the initiation rites of the new tribal system. It didn't matter what you learned, if anything, the only important thing was that you reached the 'hallowed grounds'. As with C. Shreber. He was a dull man who had written a dull book, and then required his students to buy the book so he could use up his classroom time explaining what he had written. Not that it didn't need explaining, she thought. And I've got this whole semester of night school to finish before I can get my degree! At least she was able to laugh at at herself, she told the school-house clock on the wall.

But as she sat over her second coffee there was a thought niggling at her mind. Why had the bulldozers gone? Certainly the wetlands scheme may have put a spoke in his wheel, but he was not the sort of man to be put off permanently. What was he up to? It had never crossed her mind that he would withdraw from the fight. There was still a ninety-day period ahead where good weather allowed building. And this had been the man she was afraid of. The man who came, fully intending to build a road, come hell or high water. Maybe that would be a help? A real high water? She laughed at her own stupid thought. Selby Brook fed the Taunton River, but it could rain forty days and forty nights and the brook wouldn't raise more than six inches of flood water. But *he* looked to be the type of man who could raise a high water just by holding up his hands! Joshua? Moses? Her memory failed her. She piled her dishes in the dishwasher, went upstairs and dressed in corded white slacks and a lace-trimmed blouse. Twenty minutes later she was off to town for her weekly shopping spree in the supermarket.

Her white Mustang was over fourteen years old, and showed a marvellous disinclination to climb the hill at Sullivan Ledge, just outside the village of Eastboro. With her usual impatience she managed to stall the motor twice before they crept over the ridge and clattered down Main Street. She went carefully into the Fernandes parking lot, fully aware of the fact that auto driving was not her best accomplishment. And in the middle of solving the mysteries of parallel parking she almost ran over her lawyer.

He was acquainted with her driving skills. He waited until she had shut off the motor before he struggled into the bucket seat beside her. As he climbed in she surveyed him; why, the old dear had spruced himself up for a Saturday morning. A lightweight grey permapress suit, a dark blue shirt, and a tie that would outsparkle the Milky Way. And a crushable white hat perched on the top of the rim of white hair that ran around the edges of his tonsured head.

'Enter, Second Conspirator, stage right,' he intoned in his best courtroom voice.

'Why Charles,' she laughed, her eyes sparkling a welcome. 'I do believe you've been—imbibing?'

'A toast, dear lady, only a toast,' he assured her. 'Two bluebirds making love at my bedroom window this morning. I owed them a toast, and the brandy bottle was convenient.'

'And then?'

'And then the bottle was empty, so I threw it at them. Noisy beggars, turning my window sill into a brothel. I hate birds! You heard, of course, that your—ah—pigeon fell right into the trap at the courthouse?'

'All because of your skill, Charles,' she lauded him. She pressed his bony arm under the lightweight coat. Not ten years ago he had been a fulsome strong man, fit to fish and farm and fight along with her husband. And now, just a bag of courtly bones. 'Was there any real trouble?' she asked.

'This one's smarter than the average,' the lawyer admitted. 'And I made a classic mistake. I pointed out the omission to the court a great deal faster than would be normal.'

'So then what happened?'

'Nothing, really—and that's what bothers me.' It wasn't usual for Charles Momson to be indecisive. She waited patiently while he thought it out. 'He came over to me and shook my hand, Mary. He wasn't angry—and he should have been. That was a low blow. Then he went back to the Bench and asked for a court order to allow his people to inspect this so-called wetland area. I told the judge that trespassing strangers would upset the cows, but I guess he had heard that one before. Anyhow, he granted the order. So I suspect that he'll be at you pretty quickly. Which ploy do we use next?'

'I think the one about the cemetery, Charles. You have all that data, don't you?'

'Yes, of course, my dear. Well, you buzz off to your shopping. I need to go down to the Legion hall and—well . . .'

'And find a few more birds to salute?' she teased. He smiled back at her, levered himself up out of the bucket seat, and tipped his hat.

All of which had her mentally contending with the troublesome Mr Latimore as she scanned the lettuce, checked the roasts, and collected vegetables that the farm itself did not produce. He was even in her mind at the check-out counter, where three bags of groceries cost her ninety-nine dollars and forty-three cents, and a wince.

Outside in the parking lot again, she resolved to kill two birds with no stone at all. She pulled out of her parking space, threatening the lives of the two bagboys who were collecting shopping carts, and rattled her way down Main Street and over Spruce, to the gleaming white spire of the church. The old building was a clapboard wooden structure whose entrance and chancel dated from 1795, although later additions—some as new as 1815—dwarfed the original building. She collected her bread tins from the Parish building. Then, as usual, she walked around to the back of the church, opened the iron gate, and went into the burial grounds where all her loves lay waiting.

She puttered around the grave sites, enjoying the sun, pulling a few weeds, and re-setting the potted plants she had brought. The Colonel's marker was still glazed with newness. She had been able to afford it only during the previous spring. A tiny holder in front of it displayed the American flag, a common commemorative, replaced each year on Memorial Days by members of the Legion and the Veterans of Foreign Wars. The marker was a semi-erect stone, polished in black, and inscribed briefly, 'Henry Addison Chase, Colonel, United States Army, in his sixtieth year. Rest in peace.'

She patted the rough edges of grass around the new stone, looked across to where her mother lay, then took the few steps backward that brought her to an iron bench, set under the clump of yellow maple trees that shaded the cemetery. Once they would all have been Elm trees, she knew, but the Dutch Elm disease had long since killed off New England's towering native Elms. She closed her eyes and relaxed, and heard the voice behind her.

'I told you it was, Daddy. I told you so. Call before she leaves, Daddy. Ask her!'

Mary straightened up her shoulders and smiled over at the little girl. 'Mattie?' she called. 'How nice to see you again. And don't you look like a lovely little girl in that pretty dress.' Behind the girl she could see the looming figure of her father, but Mary's busy mind kept her from looking fully at him. She stretched out welcoming arms to Mattie, and the little girl came running down the path and into their shelter. Mary swung the child up to shoulder height, muzzling her face in the child's soft hair. It seemed almost as if Becky were a child again, the Colonel's protective shadow about them all, and the world was at peace.

'Nothing for me, Mrs Chase?' his deep voice asked.

'I'm—afraid I can't pick you up, Mr Latimore,' she returned stiffly. He had caught her with her guard down, she was flustered, and she showed it. Her face turned red, her lips tightened to a narrow line, and her eyes sparked at him. She dropped the girl to the ground gently, took six deep breaths to restore her calm, and then looked up at him. She had only one refuge. Somehow or another she must get him off balance, surprise him.

'I hardly expected to see you in such a place as this,' she said primly. 'Did you go to the court hearing?'

'Indeed I did,' he confessed ruefully. 'And your Mr Momson led us down the primrose path, let me tell you. But then I understand you never would let my men on to your land, so how could we know there was a swamp?'

'It was only on my lawyer's advice,' she lied. 'You're not angry?'

'Of course not,' he laughed, 'but don't forget—you fool me once, shame on you. You fool me twice, shame on me! I mean to build that road, Mrs Chase.'

'I know you do,' she acknowledged sadly. 'But what brings you here?'

'We were just passing by and happened to see you through the fence,' he returned. There was a smile playing around the corners of his mouth, and for some crazy reason she felt like a field mouse with the whir of the hunting owl overhead, almost subconsciously she ducked. He broke out laughing. He knows what I'm thinking, she told herself. Or is he reading my face? She made an effort to restore the normally placid look to her face.

'What I meant was what are you doing in Eastboro?' She had all her antennae out now. Eyes on his face, ears intent for every change in his voice, and her busy mind poised to analyse all the incoming data.

'Oh that. I thought you knew. Small town gossip, and all that.'

'We moved!' Mattie interrupted. 'We don't live in Boston no more, Mrs Chase. Ask her, Daddy.'

'Wait now, princess,' he said. 'One step at a time please.'

'Ask me what?' Mary prompted.

'We—Mattie and I, that is—thought that the rest of the summer in the country would be—healthful, so to speak.'

'And he fired Mrs Driscoll and bought us a house

just on the other side of the church and we're going to live there all summer, just the two of us, only we got a problem, Mrs Chase,' the little girl stopped to catch her breath, then looked up at Mary with the most appealing blue eyes she had ever seen. Mary found it hard to tear herself away from the tiny bundle of wistfulness at her knee, but alarm bells were ringing in her ears. He had bought a house in Eastboro, and moved in already! Why? To make sure that his road got built? To keep a close personal eye on whoever it was that was delaying the construction? What other reason could there be? While she stood still, mind a blank, he wandered over to the gravesite and poked around with a casual foot.

'You come regularly, I suppose,' he asked casually. 'That's something we don't see much of in the big city these days.'

'I try to come once a week,' she responded. 'That's my mother's grave in the corner.' He walked over and checked the tiny stone. 'She died eleven years ago?' he asked. Mary nodded. He started to walk back to her, and then stopped. 'Well, at least you weren't alone,' he said quietly. 'You had your grandfather with you until five years ago.'

'My grandfather?' He might as well have slapped her face. He was standing idly by her husband's headstone and remarking it as her grandfather's. Damn him! In the village, where everyone knew the circumstances, there was never a cutting remark, a hurtful word. But here was this—stranger—stabbing her to death with his tongue!

Fumbling through misty eyes she gathered up her bread tins, her potting shears, and her water bucket, and strode off down the path towards the gate. She had not really cried over Henry in three years. But now the tears came, little droplets, one at a time from each eye, running down her cheeks. She could hear his footsteps behind her. They served to speed her on her way.

'What happened, Daddy? What did you say?' Mattie
cried out behind her.

'I don't know, dammit!' He was almost up to her. Her
hands reached out for the latch on the gate, but when
she pulled back to open it, his strength was pledged
against hers, and the old iron gate remained closed.

'Let me go,' she muttered through the sobs.

'What did I say?' he persisted. 'I didn't——'

She turned her back on him, fumbling in her shoulder
bag for a handkerchief. Mattie came running up in
front of her, threw her little arms around Mary's waist,
and offered comfort without words. Mary dropped her
hand on to the silky skein of the child's hair, and the
tears were stemmed. She wiped at both eyes with her
soaked handkerchief, sniffed back the last two droplets,
and offered them a tentative small smile.

'What was it you wanted to ask me?' she enquired.

'Afterwards,' he rumbled. 'He wasn't your grandfather?'

'No.'

'Mrs Chase, how old were you when you married?'

Her head snapped back as she searched his face.
There was no message, just that predatory gleam in the
hooded eyes. 'I was seventeen,' she retorted. 'And how
old were you when you married, Mr Latimore?'

'I was—oh, I see. I'm sorry, Mrs Chase. I'm not too
diplomatic today, am I?' He didn't appear to be
particularly hurt by the admission. What in the world is
he up to? Her usually logical mind was running in
circles. Think carefully, Mary Chase, she commanded
herself. There's too much at stake to let emotions
interfere. Too much at stake for both Becky and Henry.

'What was it you wanted to ask me?' she repeated.
Her hand was on one of the spiked iron staunchions
that made up the wrought iron fence, she needed the
support badly, her knees were trembling.

There was another bench just beyond the gate. He

helped her through, and almost thrust her down on to the seat. 'You look pale,' he commented. 'You'd better sit down before you fall down.'

'I'm all right,' she insisted. 'What is it?'

He sat down beside her, and suddenly the spacious bench became too crowded. His thigh was against hers, bringing a warmth that she had long since forgotten. And something else that she wanted to forget! He stretched one arm behind her along the back rest of the bench. The top of her head came only to his shoulder, she noticed suddenly. I'd need a stepladder to rest my head on his shoulder—if I wanted to. If I wanted to? There was only one answer to this complex situation. She shut down her mind, turned off all her senses, folded her hands primly in her lap, and concentrated on looking straight ahead.

'This problem,' his deep voice rumbled over her head. She nodded to show she was listening, but transferred her stare to the two shiny rocks that glittered in the path at her feet. 'Mattie and I are all moved in,' he continued, 'but our housekeeper won't be able to come until Wednesday. And tomorrow I have to fly back to Venezuela for one last inspection of the dam we are building there. Which leaves me with the problem of what to do with Mattie. She absolutely refuses to go back to the Driscolls. All she can talk about is Becky and Mrs Chase. So I wondered, Mrs Chase——'

'If she could stay with us for a few days?'

'Well, I had hoped that you might be willing to come down and stay with her in our new house?'

'No. That would be impossible,' she sighed. 'Somerfield Farms is my home. Has been my home since I was twelve years old. But certainly Mattie would be welcome to stay at the farm with us. The only problem would be Tuesday night. I go to Boston every Tuesday and Friday night, to a school, you know. But I'm sure that if Becky isn't free, we could have Anna and Henry watch out for her. Yes, of course she can come. And stay as long as she likes.'

The little girl whooped with glee, dancing around her two adults and their bench as if they were the laagered wagon train, and she the Apache Nation. 'That's enough of that,' he snapped. 'Remember where we are!'

Mattie kept on dancing and whooping until Mary leaned out in her way, caught at her wrist, and brought her to a halt. 'That's enough, missy,' she said softly, and the child grew quiet.

'How in the world did you do that?' He was puzzled. 'Mrs Driscoll never could control her.'

'You said it the other day,' she reminded him. 'I'm a witch. When will you bring her to us?'

'Tonight?' he suggested. 'My flight leaves from Logan at midnight.'

'Yes, do that,' Mary said. 'And come early—about six o'clock. We'll have supper together. You and I, Becky and Mattie.'

'That would be nice,' he chuckled. 'Babysitting and a free home-cooked meal!'

'I'm not a baby, Daddy.'

'No, of course you aren't,' he replied. 'Anybody can tell by looking at you that you're over six years old. It's easy to see. I wish I could tell the ages of other women just by looking at them.'

'If you're hinting about me,' Mary chuckled, 'I can save you a deal of worrying. I'm over six too.' The look he gave her indicated no appreciation of her humour. She smiled wryly at him, then bent down to the child. 'Dress pretty for supper,' she whispered to her. 'Becky and I love to get all gussied up on Saturday night. Promise?'

The little head nodded and smiled. 'It's a secret?' she asked.

'It's a girl-type secret,' Mary confirmed. 'Tonight, by six o'clock. Don't forget to bring your daddy.'

'What in the world are you two conspiring about?' he asked.

'Girl-talk,' his daughter told him. 'Men can't listen to girl-talk.' He looked as if he were about to explode so before anything desperate could happen, Mary kissed Mattie and scooted down the walk around the south side of the church, as fast as her legs could carry her.

Becky was all enthused about the supper. 'It's been a long time,' she told her stepmother, 'since we really entertained at home. Can I—could we——?'

'Harold?' Mary asked as she laid out the tenderloins, examined the marbling of the meat and rubbed in the butter. 'Why not. We'll go first class. You go call him, and then whip back here. You can make—oh—a Waldorf salad, please. We've plenty of fresh apples.'

Becky was back within five minutes. 'He'll come,' she said. 'What else besides apples in the salad?'

'Core and cut the apples,' Mary told her, 'add some finely chopped celery, mayonnaise, and lemon juice. Then garnish it with those chopped pecans we've been saving, and put it in the refrigerator till we need it.'

As she talked Mary's hands were busy working with the materials for the topping of the tournedos. She added the stems of a dozen large mushrooms to the melted butter, chopped in one shallot, and cooked the mixture over a low flame for ten minutes. Then she added flour and enough chicken stock to moisten the mixture, seasoned it with salt, pepper and fresh parsley, and set it aside.

The vegetables were already prepared in a casserole. Peas, carrots and lima beans, cooked first until tender, then moistened with mushroom soup and milk. The bread crumb and grated cheese topping she set aside for later. Becky had already finished the salad, and started on a lemon and lime sherbet, with vanilla wafers.

It was four o'clock before the both of them were able to step back from their kitchen work, shed their aprons, and move out to the living room to relax over a cup of coffee. They took turns showering, and went to dress.

'What am I doing all this for?' she asked her mirror image as she sat before her vanity table, clad only in her lacy briefs.

'You know why!' Becky shouted from next door.

'Oh do I?' she returned. Her step-daughter came around the jamb of the door, in a pale white slip.

'Because he's from the big city, and he gives the impression that we're all a bunch of hicks, and you want to give him one on the nose—or in the stomach, so to speak! You don't fool me, Ma.'

'Oh my goodness. Don't I?'

'You used to, but I'm getting smarter. I can tell you something you don't even know. Bet?'

'Bet what?'

'Bet that you like that man a lot!'

'Go on with you,' she laughed indulgently. 'He doesn't like me. He thinks, first of all, that I'm *only* a woman, and secondly that I'm an obstruction to his precious road!'

'*Only* a woman?' Becky asked. 'C'mon Ma!'

They both went downstairs at five o'clock, Mary in a calf-length silver sheath, slit up the right side almost to mid-thigh, Becky in a red calico grannie gown that swept from a high lace collar to wide, floor-length skirts. While Becky set the table, Mary went back to the kitchen, donned a long apron, and put the tenderloins in the broiler and the casserole in the oven. When they were partly broiled, she pulled them out adding the filling of mushroom stems to the large mushroom caps, covering the whole with butter and cracker crumbs. She topped each steak with a mushroom cap before popping them back into the oven. As she worked on the *velouté* sauce she heard the doorbell ring. She quickly started the wild rice, set the timers, whipped off her apron, and went out to greet the guests.

They had all arrived at once. Mattie was swirling a mid-calf yellow-sprigged dress. Her father looked casually formal in dark trousers and a tan sports coat, while Harold tried to hide himself in a corner, in his formal three-piece grey suit.

Mary made small talk easily. The Colonel had demanded it, and she had quickly learned. By six o'clock they were all relaxed, and the kitchen timers began to ring all over the house. Another idea of the Colonel's. 'Nobody stands around in the kitchen longer than necessary,' he was accustomed to say, 'and nobody burns the supper.' All of which Mary had added to the Two Hundred Commandments that governed the lives of all the Mrs Chases. One of the joys of living with the Colonel was that you always knew just where you stood.

Becky served the first course, of her own making. Hot cheese buns, and chilled shrimp bisque. As she sat at the head of the table, Mary had problems disguising her giggle. Harold looked appalled. Mr Latimore looked thunderstruck. Driven by her devils she looked across the table at him. 'Not what you expected?' she asked.

'No—not exactly,' he replied, but she noted that his implements were hard at work. 'But it does taste delicious. You're a good cook, Mrs Chase.'

'Not me,' she denied. 'Becky made all this. *She*'s a good cook. Would you prefer a hamburger, Harold?'

'Who me? No. Never,' he lied manfully as he struggled with the shrimp. 'It's good. I didn't know you could cook, Becky.'

'Not me!' Becky mocked her mother. 'I just do the leg work. Ma taught me everything, but I'm better at hamburgers.'

'But right now we'll get the main course on the table,' Mary commented. 'Mattie, you'll help?'

As the two younger girls cleared the first-course settings, Mary took the tornedoes out of the oven and brought them through on individual plates. Mattie managed the salad by herself, and Becky brought in the *casserole à la bishop,* and set it on a hot pad in the middle of the table.

Harold's face changed colours, from pale white to red. 'I didn't realise there was more,' he confessed. 'I thought the dinner was just shrimp. Boy that looks good.'

As it did, Mary told herself. She had added cherry tomatoes to the lightly browned concoction, as a decoration, and the *velouté* sauce was just right.

There was a dearth of conversation after that. Knives and forks clattered energetically until every plate was cleared, and they all sat back in their chairs and heaved a collective sigh of relief.

'I haven't eaten like that since I was a schoolboy in Paris,' Bruce Latimore commented. 'Where did you learn to cook like that?'

For some reason she felt the mad impulse to jar him out of his self-satisfied position. 'You mean how did a little country girl learn to cook like that?' she asked. His eyebrows beetled, a frown whisked across his face and was immediately buried. She was struck with a flash of remorse. 'I'm sorry,' she said humbly, 'that was rude of me. My husband was an army officer. He believed in proper training for every job. Once it was decided I would cook for the family he sent me off to a culinary school in Boston. A very methodical man, the Colonel. And yes, I can cook hamburgers too!' She dimpled a pretty smile at him and was rewarded with an eye-message that tendered full-score forgiveness. She dropped her hands into her lap, surprised. Why, how attractive he looks when he smiles, she thought.

'Ma? Ma! About the dessert, Ma.' Becky was at the far end of the table, trying to attract her attention. She snapped out of her musings. 'I was—I was thinking of something,' she apologised, getting up from her chair.

It was a matter of minutes before the sherbet was before everyone, minutes which Bruce filled by telling stories about his last trip to Venezuela, and the monkey which had beset his hut on one of the sites. Mary was walking behind dish-laden Mattie on one of the trips to the kitchen, when they met Becky coming from the other direction. Mattie had laughed so hard at her father's story that tears were running down her cheeks.

'My daddy's a wonderful man,' she announced to Becky en passant. Both the girls stopped, almost tripping Mary in the process. 'And my mother's a wonderful woman,' Becky announced. At which they both stared at each other as if sharing some secret out of Mary's ken. And then they both started laughing again, and went their separate ways.

Harold proved his training after the meal. As soon as he heard that Becky was to wash the dishes, he volunteered to assist, and the pair vanished into the kitchen.

'They only have to load the dishwasher,' Mary explained as she led Bruce off to the sitting room for coffee. He waved off her offer of a tippet of Cointreau, and settled down in the Colonel's favourite chair. He thumped the arm appreciatively.

'Fine chair,' he commented. 'Solid. Big enough to hold a coffee cup. I can't bear to have to balance a cup of anything on my knee.'

'I agree,' she laughed happily. And suddenly everything seemed so—agreeable. It was a warm August evening, and the big front windows were wide open, letting in a smell of a cooling north east breeze. And here she was, relaxing in her own sitting room, with a most comfortable man, and two fine daughters, and suddenly everything seemed to be so—well, lovable. Except that the clock was striking nine, and Mattie was struggling hard to cover her yawns. Mary set her cup down and excused them both.

It took thirty minutes to tease the little girl into and out of the tub, but in between there were some happy splashes that made her glad she had donned an apron again. Such a skinny thing, she thought, as she watched the girl duck under the soapy water. She needs feeding up—and ten thousand tons of loving!

But eventually Mattie, swathed in a long silk nightgown, was ready for bed. Mary led her into her temporary room, set a couple of books by the side of the bed, kissed her, and went downstairs.

'You'll want to read her to sleep,' she told him. He reacted as if the idea had never crossed his mind. Nevertheless he went up the stairs, and presently Mary could hear the drone of the Three Bears drifting down the stairs. She went back to the sitting room, snuggled into one of the big easy chairs, slipped off her high heel shoes, and put her tiny feet up on a hassock. By the time he returned she was almost asleep, her hair had come down in two long, blonde, untidy braids clustering around her face. She jumped, startled, when he made a small noise.

'Becky?' he asked.

'Taking a walk with Harold,' she sighed. 'I wish I were young again. My feet hurt.'

'It's those shoes,' he said as he poured himself another cup of coffee. 'You shouldn't wear such high heels.'

'I know that,' she retorted crossly. 'But I have to.'

'You could wear stilts and it wouldn't do any good,' he said blandly. 'You just have to adapt to being short, my dear.'

My dear? It had almost slipped by her. A slip of the tongue, she was positive. Even Superman could make a slip of the tongue. But it did sound so nice. Everything seemed so nice.

'I'm afraid it's the witching hour,' he said, setting his coffee cup aside. 'It's ten o'clock. It will take me almost an hour to drive to Logan, and there's a one-hour early check-in on non stop flights overseas.'

'I suppose you're right,' she said, struggling to her feet. She was still a little—sleepy? No, that wasn't really it. Bemused? Well, she could think it out later.

'I've had a marvellous time,' he was saying, and that deep voice rumbled like the opening peal of the church organ. 'But I can't go along calling you Mrs Chase?'

She blushed. 'It's been so long——' she stammered. 'I've been "Ma" for so many years. They used to call me Mary Kate.'

'That's better, Mary Kate.' She followed him to the door, where suddenly she was turned towards him, and almost engulfed in the pocket of his sports coat. 'And I can't tell you how much I appreciate your taking Mattie in hand.'

He was holding both her arms, just below the shoulders. She leaned back to get a better look at his face, suspending all her weight on his steel fingers. Come on now, Mary Kate, she chided herself, say something, quick.

'This—with Mattie staying over. This isn't a Trojan Horse, is it Mr Latimore? Is that what you really want?'

'No indeed, Mary Kate.' And now he was definitely laughing at her. 'What I really want is to kiss you.' And he did.

CHAPTER THREE

MARY stood at the door for twenty minutes, long after the tail lights of his heavy Cadillac had disappeared down the road. Her mind was musty, confused. Occasionally one of her fingers came up and gently touched her lips, but mostly she just stood and stared out into the darkness, dreaming. When one of her arms, without direction, shut the front door, she remained there, staring at the closed door for another few minutes. Then she fought her way back to reality, snapped on the back porch lights to indicate to Becky that her freedom was not limitless, and walked slowly up to her room.

She had intended to cream her face and comb her hair out. Instead, she sat down at her vanity, rested both elbows on the table top, put her chin into the protective hollow made by her hands, and spent another half hour studying herself in the mirror. What was there to be seen? Freckles? Lord, if they ever became a beauty item, she would lead the parade. Tiny, light, they ran in random sequence across the bridge of her nose and up over her cheeks to just under her eyes. A slightly brown skin she had, at least in those places not covered by her bikini. High rounded cheeks that never needed additional colour. Green, sparkling eyes that looked grey on cloudy days—or angry days. And long light brown hair. Not the light brown of his briefcase. Rather the tassel-top colour of ripened corn. Not much bait for a man-trap! She shook her head in disgust, and gave herself a lecture.

'Look at you, Mary Chase,' she said sternly. 'Twenty-seven years old. A widow. Two step-children.

A secure future. A husband whom once you loved. Why would you want another man?'

There was a clatter on the stairs, and Becky stuck her head in. 'Talking to yourself again, Ma?'

'Can't find anyone else to listen,' she returned ruefully. 'Harold gone home?'

'Yup. You were right, Ma!'

'Right what, honey?'

'He's an octopus. I think I'll fish around the pond a little more.'

'That's my girl, Becky. You do that.'

'Church tomorrow?'

'As usual, dear. You're not too tired?'

'Not to worry, Ma. I can out-wrestle a guy his size three times a day! Now if it were Mr Latimore—well, that would be different. Did you do any wrestling with him?'

'Becky!'

'Okay, Ma, but it might be fun!' The girl ducked as a pillow smacked into the door frame where she had been standing, then she went off to her own room. But through the open doors Mary could hear the giggling continue until the bedsprings creaked.

Wrestling with him! Indeed! But maybe—she looked into the mirror again, and found that her hands had been undressing her, without telling her brain anything about the matter, and she now stood nude before the unlying glass. She stopped for just the tiniest peek—just the tiniest. Her right hand gently stroked herself, from rounded thigh to the pointed peak of her ample breast. Even her own touch bothered her—called up too many sensations long buried, until finally she became aware of where her senses were leading her. She snatched her hand back, grabbed a robe, and ran for a cold cold shower.

Monday was a nice day, for all that she hadn't slept a wink the entire weekend. Mattie was up early. Becky slept in, and at about ten o'clock in the morning two casually dressed men appeared at the front door.

'From the Latimore Corporation,' they introduced themselves. 'We have a court order permitting us to view the so-called wetlands on Somerfields Farms. Is it okay if we go ahead?'

'Yes, of course,' she said. She stepped out on the porch and gestured up the hill behind the house. 'That's Blueberry Hill,' she pointed out, smiling. 'On the other side you'll find a so-called brook and an alleged spring. And if you follow them down the hill, you'll find a so-called swamp area. And please be careful. If you fall into the so-called swamp you will very definitely get wet!'

They both grinned back at her, big broad grins from big broad construction men. 'Don't worry, lady,' the leader said. 'We had a long, long talk with Mr Latimore before we came out here. We understand completely.'

'And you realise that the court order does not give you permission to explore any other area except the wetlands—I beg your pardon, the so-called wetlands?'

'Oh yes. We understand entirely. No spying, right?'

'Well,' she relented, 'there's no sense being sticky about it. Lunch is at twelve-thirty.'

'We brought our own bag lunch, ma'am.'

'Lunch is at twelve-thirty. Nobody eats out of bags on *my* farm!'

For three days the two men tramped the farm area, turning up dusty and tired for lunch, and then leaving promptly at five o'clock. On the last day they brought an assortment of surveying equipment with them, and out of sheer curiosity, Mary encouraged Mattie to go swimming with her. Becky, overhearing the conversation, threw up her hands and refused to join in.

'You're not going to freeze me to death,' she stated. 'I'm off for my driver's lesson this afternoon.'

'Good heavens, I had forgotten about that,' Mary

laughed. 'Of course that's the most important thing in the world. Are they picking you up here?'

'Yes, Ma. There'll be three of us and the instructor. We'll be riding around most of the afternoon, I guess. You know I only have three more lessons before I go for my test?'

'Oh, I know, I know,' her stepmother laughed. 'I just wonder if the world is ready for you. I think I'll take an ad in the Courier, disclaiming any knowledge or responsibility. How about you, Mattie. You're not taking driving lessons, are you?'

'No, I don't think so,' the little girl replied. 'I was taking piano lessons, but Mr Hart said I'd—what was it he said—something about I should be a carpenter instead of a piano player. Boy he was mad. He shouted at me, and he shouted at Mrs Driscoll. But I tell you something, he would never have shouted at Daddy!'

'Who would dare,' Mary said under her breath. 'Well, get your swim suit then, honey, and we'll go hit the old swimming hole.'

It was only a fifteen minute walk from the house to the swimming site. Mattie chattered all the way, her tongue seizing on every new thing that her eyes discovered.

Selby Brook, and the spring which was its source, had been dammed at the bottom of the narrow gully between two hills, and a pool of water, about twice the size of an Olympic swimming pool, established. But as Mattie quickly found out, a swimming hole fed by cold spring water which was in continual flow over the dam and into the surrounding swamp, could never compare to the warmth of a pool whose trapped waters could gain some heat from the sun. Despite Mary's warning the child dived in and promptly did a racing sprint for the opposite side, where she climbed out.

'It gets better after you move around a bit,' Mary called to her. She shed her robe, poised for a moment

on the wide flat top of the dam, and dived in. After
watching guardedly for a few minutes, Mattie joined
her, and the two raced and played for a time, before
coming out to rest on the grass verge on the south side
of the pool.

'You swim like a little fish,' Mary assured the girl.
'Did you take lessons?'

Mattie was sitting in the V of Mary's legs, while her
hair was being vigorously towelled. 'Oh did I ever,' the
little girl replied. 'You know—they had everything to
keep me busy. Don't let Mathilda get bored—that's
what they always said. But I like swimming. It's not like
playing the piano, or anything. I like it.'

Mary finished drying the child's hair. It already
seemed longer than when first the Latimores had come
to the farm, and was well on its way to becoming a cap
of tightly interwoven curls. Mary combed it out for her,
then turned to her own tangled matt. Mattie patted her
head and smiled complacently. 'That's nice,' she said.
'Mrs Driscoll never did anything like that. She said
every kid has gotta do for theirselves—themselves.
Whatever.'

'Whatever,' Mary agreed solemnly. 'What else did
she say?'

'I don't remember exactly what. But it all started with
don't! You don't never say don't to Becky, do you?'

'Not now,' Mary chuckled. 'But once or twice when
she was your age I did. There are things a girl shouldn't
do, and sometimes it's hard to explain them. But Becky
trusted me. I suspect Mrs Driscoll had a lot of reasons
for saying don't.'

'No, I don't think so. I think she said don't 'cause she
liked to say it. She liked to be mean. She's not like you.
Not at all like you.'

'Oh well, now, I can't imagine that she wanted—not to
like you, Mattie. Here, come around and sit beside me
now, and let the sun dry you off. There's a good girl.'

'You know, you're very soft, Mz Chase? Did you know that?'

'You mean I ought to go on a diet?'

'No! Don't do that! Daddy said——Well, that was the second thing. The first thing that Daddy said was don't you ever tell Mz Chase about that!'

'Aha. A family secret, huh?'

'I guess so. You know that Glenda Hawkins hugged me once? She didn't want to, but Daddy was watching, so she did. She's all bones, she is. She's a lot bigger than you, but bones, you know. I didn't like to hug her. And her and Daddy——'

'She and Daddy, dear.'

'Yes. She and Daddy, they had one great big smashing fight, let me tell you? She threw Daddy's favourite pipe in the fireplace, and broke it, and then she kicked the lamp over, and——'

'I—I don't think you ought to be telling me this, Mattie. So Mattie stands for Mathilda, does it? That's a nice name.'

'It's my grandmother's name. She lives in Newport. Did you ever live in Newport?'

'Me? No, I went there once on a visit. Just for a few days.'

They sat in companionable silence for a while, Mary watching the distant figures of the two surveyors, hard at work. The little girl nestled close to her, and eventually stretched out with her head on Mary's lap. 'You know something,' she said after a while. 'I could help you.'

Mary smiled. She was paying only one ear's worth of attention. 'Of course you can. How?' she asked.

'Well, you got a nice daughter, but she's growing old, you know.'

'Becky? Old? I suppose, now that you mention it, fifteen is getting along. But I still think of her as very young, Mattie.'

'I don't see how you can,' the little girl continued doggedly. 'She's bigger than you are—well, she's taller than you are, anyway. She's getting old.'

'Hmm. If you promise not to mention it to Becky, all right, we'll accept the idea. Becky's getting old. And now what?'

'I ain't very old. In fact I'm practically new, you know.'

Mary finally turned her complete attention to the child. She tilted back the tousled little head and cuddled her. 'Yes, I can see that,' she said. 'You're practically a new model.'

'And I don't got no mother.'

'Ah!'

'And pretty soon you ain't gonna have no daughter,' and then with a rush of eager words, 'so why don't you be my mother and when Becky gets too old to be a daughter you'll have me and I'll have you and that would be a wonderful thing for both of us, don't you think?'

'Why, I—I think it would be a lovely idea, but it needs considerable thought,' she answered quietly. 'But you're certainly right. I've gotten accustomed to having a daughter, and Becky *is* getting old. But there are a number of other factors, you know. For example, we would have to consider what to do about your daddy, poppet.'

'Oh, we could keep him. He's nice to have around the house, you know. He can fix things, and lift things, and empty the garbage, and things like that.'

Mary could not restrain her giggles. And with Mattie joining in, it became a circus. Both of them rolled back and forth aggravating the situation by tickling each other, until finally it was time to go. 'But you will think about it?' the little girl persisted.

'Yes, I'll think about it,' she promised solemnly. And indeed she did, all through the long night. Bruce

Latimore, replacing her worn-out light bulbs, carrying her trunks downstairs, moving in and out of the kitchen with endless bags of garbage in his hands. Carrying my trunks down the stairs? Why? Where would I be going—with him? Now that was a thought that completely sobered her dreams. She rolled over on her stomach, buried her head beneath the pillows, and finally blanked out.

He arrived at the house at about six thirty the next morning, just as she was opening the door to collect the milk. He was tired, unshaven, with his executive tie loosened at the knot, and his executive jacket suspended over one shoulder by his thumb. She was barely dressed, with her old green robe over her short nightgown, and her hair in a wild mess.

'I'm not too early am I?' he asked as he walked up on to the porch. She could feel that peculiar excitement again, running up and down her spine as if the devil's fingers were using her backbone for an xylophone.

'Depends on what you came for,' she suggested. 'If it's breakfast, you're just in time. If it's Doomsday, I think you're a little early. And if it's road-building day, they haven't finished the survey yet!'

'Breakfast sounds great,' he returned. 'As it happens, I was talking about daughter-picking-up time. Am I too early for that?'

'Lordy are you ever. That little girl has been running her heels off for four days. She won't open an eye much before nine o'clock. How's the construction business?'

He followed her into the kitchen, scrubbing his shoes on the mat just outside the door. No doubt about it, she told herself, this man is just too good to be true. Just too well trained to be real!

'The construction business in Venezuela is pretty good,' he admitted as he dropped his coat over the back of one of the kitchen chairs. 'Around these parts I understand it's not so good.'

'Oh?' she said, hoping he would be more forthcoming, and not daring to ask outright. 'Scrambled eggs? Toast? Bacon? Ham? Cereal? Orange juice?'

'Yes,' he responded. 'And coffee. About two gallons of it.'

She turned around to look at him, arching her eyebrows. 'You mean you want *everything* I said?'

'Of course,' he replied, 'I'm a growing boy. Would you mind hurrying?' He leaned across the table and picked up the day's copy of the *Boston Globe*. She watched him out of the corner of her eyes as she worked. Typical male, she thought, as she cracked four eggs and swirled them up with a clean fork. Order breakfast, pick up the paper, and turn right away to the sports page. He thinks this is a Howard Johnsons! She separated six slices of bacon and added them to the griddle-top of the gas stove. And then, having second thoughts, pulled out the half-eaten shoulder of ham from the refrigerator, and cut off four thick slices. Toast! What did I do with the sliced bread—oh, here it is. She dropped four slices into the double toaster. And in my own home, for goodness' sakes. Giving me orders as if it were a restaurant, when we both know that I'm the Good Guys and he's the Bad Guys. That's what the Colonel always said. If you intend to fight, make sure you have designated the enemy!

'You know, you really surprised me when I walked up to the house,' he said. 'There you were bringing in the milk.'

'And in my oldest clothes,' she laughed. 'But what's so surprising about that?'

'What's so surprising? You've got over two hundred cows out there, and you have to get your milk from a dairy truck?'

'Oh that! But you see, the milk doesn't come from the cow already pasteurised. And besides, those are Henry's cows, not mine. He runs a milk business. I'm just a customer.'

'Oh? For some reason I thought you owned the whole farm.'

'You thought I was the rich Mrs Chase? Does that explain all your sudden attention?' His face darkened, and his eyes turned cold. 'Oh, I *am* sorry Mr Latimore. I meant it as a joke—a very poor one, I can see. Actually, the farm was left half to Henry, and half to Becky, with Becky's share in my trust until she is eighteen, or marries.'

'Now I see,' he said, ducking behind the paper again 'Don't forget to turn on the coffee pot.'

She was about to make a pointed comment, but at that moment the toast popped up and she had not the nerve to hand it to him cold or unbuttered. So the moment passed, but not the deed. She marked it down in her memory box under M for 'murder'. She was still muttering under her breath when she slapped the loaded plate down in front of him, and almost scalded him when the coffee mug slopped over on the table. He folded up the paper, and laid it carefully beside the plate.

'Not bad,' he commented, scanning the overloaded plate. 'But you could easily have broken it, you know!'

'I'll bet I could,' she muttered. Right over your head. You came within an ace of being decorated with the Egg of the Month. By now her temper was bubbling so high that she decided to offer him the ultimate insult. She reached into the refrigerator, pulled out a bottle of ketchup, and set it by his plate. He looked up at her with a broad grin on his face

'When I see ham I want to taste ham,' he said. 'I only use ketchup when I find the cook has ruined the food.'

Which was so exactly in agreement with her own thoughts on the matter that she broke out laughing, fetched another mug for coffee for herself, and sat down to watch him manoeuvre his way through the meal. It was—pleasurable—to sit opposite him, nursing her mug of coffee, watching his mobile face change from surprise to delight to concern as they made small talk.

'But Mattie wasn't a problem?' he persisted, having come back three times to the same subject.

'Of course not,' she assured him. 'She went into some sort of partnership with Becky, and they had a good time. They get along well together.'

'Partnership?'

'Yes. We have chickens, you know. They all belong to Becky. She takes care of them, feeds them, gathers the eggs, markets—everything having to do with chickens, Becky does.'

'She likes chickens?'

'No. She hates chickens. But she likes money, and the independence it brings. I expect she'll get her driver's licence on her next birthday, and she's saving to buy a car. Her brother Henry is a good mechanic so he's helping her to make her choice.'

'And that's the core of it, I suppose? The way you've brought her up? Responsibilities, respect, religion, independence?'

'I—I guess you could say that, yes. We all need those things, don't we? But not just that. Also love and sharing. Especially love. Tell me about the construction business around here?'

'It's a matter of weather and priorities,' he said. He had gulped the last of the eggs, the dry cereal, the ham and was now working on his second cup of coffee. 'We make our profits from the maximum use of equipment. Most of our heavy stuff is working on a highway bypass out near Fitchburg. We can hardly do much outside work in Massachusetts after the fifteenth of October. So if we can't start here by the first of October, we won't be able to start at all until spring. That's why I'm pushing my surveyors on this wetlands thing. I hope we'll work up the report for the court by the first of September—ten more days—and that will still give us thirty days to whip things into shape.'

'You really mean that?' she gasped. 'We won't harvest the experimental corn until September. You'd ruin all our crops?'

'It can't be as bad as all that!' He was laughing at her, his mouth wide, with crinkles around the eyes. Sitting in her kitchen, his stomach warmed by her food, talking calmly about ruining all the year's work in a matter of weeks! And laughing about it, as if it were a game. The Colonel was right! To conduct a good fight you had to have an enemy! And here she was, sitting and gossiping with the arch-fiend of all time!

'I hope you won't be offended, Mr Latimore,' she said stiffly, 'if I wish you bad luck with your schedules.'

'Totally understood,' he said, sweeping her with a one-sided smile. 'And by the way, that lawyer of yours. I want to——'

'You mean Mr Momson?'

'Yes, that's the fellow. You realise I hope that you are walking a thin edge in this court case. Momson's so old he can hardly keep awake in court. And he drinks. Did you know that?'

She tried to suck in her breath, as if surprised, but it was hard work to keep from laughing. 'You really mean that? Mr Momson drinks?'

'You'd better believe it. Last week he was taking a nip here and there throughout the whole court session. You'd better have a look around for another lawyer.'

'How nice of you to think of us that way,' she said quietly. So Charley Momson drank a little? And might fail them at the Bar? Her smile kept sneaking out the corners of her mouth, and required ruthless extermination. She could remember the days—not too many of them in the latter days—when Charley and the Colonel had celebrated by drinking most of the community under the table. After which Charley would look around, straighten his coat and tie, and go merrily off for a full day in court.

'I do know about Charley's—problem——' she told him. 'And we're working hard to qualify another lawyer to take his place. Someone a little younger, of course.' Me, for example, she wanted to yell at him. It takes five years at night school, and I'll graduate next April, and sit for the Bar exam in May. And if poor Charley, with his weak heart, his forty percent military disability, and his failing memory, can hold on that long, we'll do you in, Mr High and Mighty Latimore!

He was still laughing at her. Those deep-hooded eyes were gleaming at her as if—'I don't want you to misunderstand, Mrs Chase,' he chuckled. 'I've been watching Mr Momson give his virtuoso performance. He's a deep one. Obviously never comes to court without two or three arrows in his quiver. No, I'm not really criticising his drinking. I feel the way President Lincoln felt when they told him General Grant was a drinker! I want to find out what Momson's brand is, so I can get some for *my* lawyers. But now, if you don't mind, I have a million things to do. If you would kindly call my daughter?'

Mattie was overjoyed to see her father. She jumped down the stairs three at a time, and vaulted into his arms with an enthusiasm that seemed to surprise him. After her breakfast, accompanied by a recall of her total experience, they had gone hand in hand down to the parked car. Mary Kate stayed in the doorway, bolstered by Becky, until the vehicle had slipped out of sight.

'Now quick, love,' she said to the girl at her side. 'On the phone. Set us up an emergency meeting of the Board. We need Henry, Mr Momson, and both of us. As quick as can be!'

'Are we in trouble again, Ma?'

'Not any more so than before. But this man's too

sharp—too sharp. He told me something about construction—something he wanted me to know. And for the life of me I can't see *why*. That's what bothers me about that man. His *whys* are always hidden so deep. Now skip, love!'

While Becky was telephoning, Mary Kate turned back to the housework, because with her fingers busy at routine tasks, her mind could range as far as she would let it, all unfettered.

The two men arrived at eleven o'clock, just as she had finished turning out the spare bedroom that Mattie had used. She went downstairs to find a quiet trio waiting for her, as well as the inevitable coffee pot not quite through its automatic perking cycle. She gestured them all to seats, and sank down into the couch, a little tired. Becky poured the coffee to taste as she scanned them all. They're all such big people, she mused. What am I doing in this crowd of big people? If Henry were to trip and fall over on me, I'd be squashed to apple butter. And if Mr Latimore were to fall over me—fall for me? Mr Latimore? He can't see me for dust!

'Ma? You going to start the meeting?' Henry was looking at her in the same way he looked at cows whose milk production was falling off.

'She's daydreaming again, Henry. I told you,' Becky said. 'Ever since that guy——'

'He has a name, Becky,' she admonished.

'Yeah. Ever since that guy Latimore came around. And now he's living in the village. Did you know that, you two? Why would a big shot like Mr Latimore come to live in our village? And you like him, don't you, Ma?'

'There,' Henry said, as if he had come to some weighty conclusion. 'That's what Anna said. You like this guy, do you, Ma?'

'Well really,' she snapped back at them. 'Just what are you implying? I like the little girl. I like her very much, but her father is an overgrown domineering arrogant sarcastic—man!'

'Ah,' Momson laughed. 'In other words he's just like the Colonel!'

'No! No indeed!' She could hardly disguise the blush that spread across her cheeks. 'Behind all the bluster the Colonel was a sincere, loving, kind man.'

'Hey,' Henry interjected, 'Anna and I have talked this over very carefully. Becky's fifteen, the farm is paying well, and you're only twenty-seven. You're at the shank of life. You've given us a lot, and none of us would be unhappy if you snatched at the gold ring on the merry-go-round again. He seems to be a nice fellow.'

'He's a road-builder,' she said bleakly. 'Now, to business.'

They all sat up and glued their eyes on her. Calling my troops to attention, she lectured herself. Don't do that. You're not the Colonel, and they're not the infantry. She sighed and folded her hands in her lap as she talked.

'For some reason that I don't understand,' she said, 'Mr Latimore has chosen to give me some information. I don't know why, but I'm sure it's not an accident. You listen, and then we'll talk. First, he's moved all his heavy equipment out to Fitchburg on another job. Second, he says he is rushing his survey of the wetlands, hoping to be back in court before the first of September. Next, he told me that after October 15th all road construction in this area will be halted for the winter. And then he said that he expects to get a court order to proceed and will definitely start work on the first of September, and be finished by the 30th. Now, why did he tell me this, and what should we do about it? Becky?'

'I'm not sure, Ma. Don't you think he's telling us that if he doesn't get started in September we'll be home clear until spring?'

'Perhaps. But I think he's a devious sort of person. Suppose that's what he wants us to think, but it's not true? Suppose he's just trying to lull us into a sense of security—a feeling that we don't have to run around digging up new facts. We could all battle him until, say, September 15th, and then sit back looking fat, dumb, and happy, and then all of a sudden, boom! And he blows us all away. I'm very suspicious. Henry?'

'Do you suppose he's telling us, rather obliquely, to get the harvest in right away? We could do it, you know. The hybrid corn will be ready in a week. The hay—well, that's sort of off and on, but we could begin almost at once on the south forty.'

'I don't know whether he was telling us that or not, but it's not a bad idea. You seem to think he has some good intention towards us. I'd *like* to believe it, but! Let's come back to that, Charley?'

'A man of many distinctions, my dear Mary,' the old lawyer mused. 'I don't remember when I've had so much fun—well, certainly not since I gave up handling sex cases in court. Now, let me see. First, you needn't worry about the crops. State law prohibits taking of land until after standing crops are harvested. Triple damages, the law allows.'

'Don't worry. He'd pay,' Mary Kate said sadly.

'Well, perhaps. Now, let me see. He's hurrying the survey. A suspicious mind like mine would lead me to wonder: if he hurries the survey, something is bound to be overlooked, what could it be? Something in the swamp? Or at least something he *thinks* is in the swamp? But then why would he tell us, unless Becky's original comments are correct?'

'Nonsense,' Mary snapped. 'I mean—why would he do that? I just don't know. Do I hear any recommendations?'

'Oh come on, Ma,' Henry laughed. 'Ever since you started studying law you've been acting like the Great

Parliamentarian. You're the boss. We know it, and you know it. Give out the marching orders.'

'I—you make me feel very embarrassed, Henry. I'm not your father, and I can't stand in his shoes. But well, this business about dates. If we can stall him off until the, say, end of September, we might have a peaceful winter. Second, I think it might be a wise thing to get the crops in early, if you can do it, Henry. Third, Charley, I think you had better prepare a brief about the cemetery. By the way, he took great fun in telling me that my lawyer was too old, too tired, and too drunk to handle my affairs. Do you suppose he knows that you were a State Supreme Court Judge before you retired.'

'I can't say about that,' the old lawyer laughed, 'but I can tell you that he's making the village rounds, listening to all the gossip, and asking a lot of pointed questions, Mary!'

'Oh dear,' she sighed. 'What sort of questions?'

'About you and the Colonel, and your relationship to Becky and Henry. And I know he was down at the newspaper office, looking through their back files for the past ten years.'

'Oh dear,' she sighed again. 'Does that mean he has some plan he's working on, or is it just "know your enemy" sort of material?' They all shook their heads at her, and then another thought struck. 'Snail-darters!' she exclaimed. 'Henry, do you think you could find us a—I don't know what you call it—a fellow who studies insects and fishes and that sort of thing?'

'I'm sure I can. In fact, I think we could get five or six students and a professor from Bridgewater State College. What do you want them to do?'

'I want to find out exactly what flora and fauna and whatever that live in our swamp. Every single kind of living thing. We might possibly really have him this time!'

'What in the world are you talking about,' Henry asked. 'What have snail-darters got to do with our swamp?'

Mr Momson was beaming heartily, as if proud of one of his pupils. 'Your mother is looking for a legal precedent,' he explained. 'Snail-darters are tiny fish that live in only one place in the world, and somebody decided to build a dam right at that spot. The Supreme Court held that since the dam might wipe out the snail-darter population of the world, that construction had to stop permanently, and no dam could ever be used at that site! Good work, my dear.'

When they all went off on their separate ways, Mary turned back to housekeeping again, and let her brain wander until the clock struck three and it was time, according to her relentless schedule to sit down with her notes, and try to make some sense out of applications of English Common Law to modern life in Massachusetts.

On Thursday she got up early because the blueberries were ripe in the swamp, and while Henry assigned two of his men to clean the bushes, Mary spent a hot day in the kitchen, steam-sanitising the glass jars, and putting up the crop for winter pies and muffins. The job lasted over into Friday, and part of Saturday. When Sunday came she was glad to sleep a little late. She dressed carefully in her lightweight, blue summer suit, and headed off to church with Becky, Henry and Anna as her escorts.

There was time for a little gossip on the steps of the church before the service, and the pastor, giving the heat of the day as a reason, cut his sermon to thirty minutes. Which was about twenty minutes more than Mary Kate could stand on this particular day. She had noticed, just before the Collect, that Bruce Latimore and Mattie were sitting in the pews directly across the aisle from her, and both of them were totally ignoring the word from the pulpit, and were staring at her.

The unwarranted attention made her squirm in her seat. Or did until Becky leaned over to her and whispered, 'What's the matter, Ma?' At which point she got the feeling that the entire congregation was looking at her condemningly! She slumped down low against the back of the old oak pew, trying to sink out of sight, but to no avail. At the conclusion of the closing hymn she debated whether to hurry out, and miss the pair across the aisle, or wait until the church had emptied. Lacking a real decision, she held to her seat until half the congregation had gone up the aisle, and then got up.

The pair across the aisle matched her timing, moved out of their pew, and followed her up the worn carpet. Becky and Mattie held a whispered conversation, but Bruce was wearing a frown, dark as night, on his face, and ignored them all. About halfway up the aisle little Mattie slipped her warm sticky fingers into Mary's, and there was a little giggle behind them. When they reached the arch of sunshine at the broad double doors, Latimore clapped on his hat, pulled Mattie away from her, said 'Mrs Chase,' in an undertaker's tone of voice, and walked away. When they were about ten paces apart, Mattie turned around, still being towed by her tall regal father, and winked an eye at Mary.

'And what do you suppose that was all about?' she mused to Becky.

'Mattie said she's been talking to her father all weekend,' Becky chortled, 'telling him what a wonderful mother you are, and how some lucky man is going to snatch you up almost any minute!'

CHAPTER FOUR

THE week that followed was grumble-week for Mary Kate. Nothing turned out right. The four apple pies she baked on Monday night were inedible because she had forgotten the sugar. At her Tuesday night law class, when the lecturer asked for quotations about the law and lawyers, all she could think of was Henry IV, and without thinking, she blurted out Shakespeare's classic comment, 'The direst thing we do, let's kill all the lawyers!' Which broke up the class, and left her shrinking in her seat for the rest of the night. On Wednesday Becky came back from her driving test with tears in her eyes, and Mary snapped at her. On Thursday the group of students who had been classifying life in the swamp turned in their report, with pictures, but she was too tired to read it. By Thursday night she was so totally down in the dumps that she forced herself to stop and reason out the whys of it all.

It took hardly any time at all. Her problem went straight back to that scene in the church when he had so palpably snubbed her as to make it painful. Painful? Who was it that babysat his daughter for four days? Me! Who was it that fed him enough breakfast for four? Me! And so what does he do? He snubs me in church! And I'll bet that that little snip of gossip was all over the town by Sunday nightfall! She brought herself up short. After all, there was no need to get nasty about it, even to yourself! And she didn't have a doubt about the gossip. She had heard two versions herself, and Becky had brought back another from the village drugstore. 'And with just that little incident I let myself in for a miserable week,' she sighed. The nerve of that man! The nerve of me! And to top it all off, I took it out on Becky. Snap out of it, Mary Chase. You'd think you were—oh, my God—falling in love? Nonsense!

When Becky came home that night from the village's only movie show, she was surprised to find her mother waiting for her with Coke and cakes and ice-cream, as well as considerably more sympathy about her driver's test.

'But I don't really feel bad about flunking the test, Ma,' she hastened to explain. 'I was mad. You bet I was. But I got over it. Imagine, he flunked me because I pulled away from the curb without making a signal. How was I to know that a truck had just come around the corner behind me? Aren't they supposed to blow a horn or something? Or not drive so fast?'

To all of which Mary was marvellously supportive, comforting, and just a little over-eager. Which Becky, not being the slowest wit in the world, noticed quietly, and stored away in her own little mental information file. The next morning, the last Friday in August, and the end of the final week of school vacation, Mary came downstairs to discover Becky talking up a storm on the telephone. Mary's mind was still on something—someone—else, so she paid little attention to the fact that her entrance into the living room halted the conversation. In fact, all she heard was Becky's last words. 'Oops. Gotta stop talking. Don't forget.' And the telephone was hung up.

'Don't let me disturb you, darling,' Mary told her. 'Who were you talking to?'

'Mattie,' her step-daughter returned. 'They've got a phone now, and she wanted to talk to me about a—about a school project she's working on.'

'For school? But it doesn't open until Wednesday. The first Wednesday after Labor Day. Don't you remember?'

'Oh, I remember. She just wants to get an early start.'

'I see.' She didn't, but it would hardly be polite to pursue the subject. She wandered off to the kitchen, still in a partial daze.

Friday night's class was a total loss. In some manner the lecturer had got his hands on the summary of the Somerfield Farms case, and had made his comments, showing very plainly, at least to Mary, that he hadn't the slightest idea what it was all about. By the time she managed to struggle through the traffic on Route 24 she was tired—bone tired. Becky was upstairs in bed. But there was a note propped up by the telephone. She left it until she had changed into her nightgown, and collected a cup of coffee from the kitchen, and a stalk of celery. She collapsed in the love-seat by the telephone, managed a sip of coffee, and picked up the note. In Becky's unformed hand it said, *Mr Latimore called. He would like to visit tomorrow night about eight o'clock. He said it was a personal matter*. She drank the rest of her coffee slowly, eyes glued to the paper. What in the world could he want? Personal? Damn the man, why couldn't he be more specific! She glanced up at the clock, which told her that it was far too late to make calls demanding explanations about what *personal* meant. So instead, she and her celery stalk plodded upstairs, stripped, wandered into the bathroom for a warm shower, and then back to her bedroom. With only two women living in the house she had long since given up the worry about robes and mules and privacy. So she wore her bath towel as a short skirt wound around her waist, and was startled when she saw her reflection in the vanity mirror. With her hair still up in a towel-turban her exposed face looked gaunt, tired. Even her shoulders seemed to be sloping, worn. 'You're suffering from the near-thirty droops,' she whispered at her reflection. Only her breasts, firm, full, cherry-tipped, were standing the test of time. She sighed as she sat down at the vanity, then broke out laughing. Somebody—Becky—had cut out a little verse from the newspaper and slipped it in the corner of her mirror. 'Mirror, mirror on the wall,' it said, 'Don't you ever lie at all?' And so to bed.

Saturday morning she slept late—for her. It was almost eight-thirty before she wandered, bleary-eyed, downstairs and into the kitchen. With only one eye open she fumbled at the coffee pot, and drew back with an expletive when she found that it was not only plugged in, but also hot. She brushed her hair back out of her eyes and tried valiantly to come awake.

'Oh Ma, you do look a fright,' Becky said from right behind her. Mary fumbled at the belt of her old green robe, and turned around, ready to be nasty.

'No, you don't catch me with that one,' the girl snickered. 'I don't intend to talk to you until you get a cup of coffee under your belt!'

'I'll belt you,' she muttered, but there was a gleam of humour in her voice. Even the Colonel had not dared to approach her until after she had had her first cup of coffee. She went through the routine mechanically. Pour until the mug was almost full. Add a shot of skimmed milk. Let it sit for two minutes. Try a sip, and discover it's too hot to drink. Add another shot of milk. Sit down at the table and nurse the mug. Then pluck up the nerve to drink it down. Her routine never changed. Except that, normally, there was nobody at the breakfast table to talk to.

'Okay,' she muttered. 'Now, why are you here at this ungodly hour, and what makes you such a smart-mouth?'

'I've got a steady job,' Becky announced, ignoring the rest of the question. 'Every Saturday. Isn't that something?'

'Yes, that's fine. Where, what, with whom, and why?'

'Boy, whatever happened to the trusting mother

routine?' Becky laughed and threw up her hands in self-defence as Mary slammed her mug down on the table. 'Okay, I surrender. I've got an all-day babysitting job down in the village. From nine o'clock until four. Every Saturday. At the minimum wage, too. Three dollars and sixty cents an hour! How about *them* potatoes.'

'And after all the taxes we paid for your education, that's what we get? How about *them* potatoes? With whom?'

'That's a joke, Ma. Just a joke. With Mr Latimore, that's whom.'

'Sitting with Mattie?'

'What else? She happens to be the only child he's got.'

'Well, that's good to know. I mean about the job, not the child. But—I wish you wouldn't take money from Mr Latimore, Becky. He—I—you know we're enemies.'

'Come off it, Ma. Antagonists, sure. Not enemies. It doesn't mean the same thing!' And with that she bustled out of the room. Moments later Mary heard her cycling down the drive, whistling.

She grumbled her way back to her coffee cup, refilling from the pot and nursing the dregs until nine-thirty. For the rest of the day she seemed to blow hot and then cold. One minute she would be on top of the world, singing, the next deep in the doldrums. By one o'clock she had got so tired of her own company that she changed into her oldest pair of jeans, with blouse to match, and went out into the kitchen garden behind the house. If the hilled potatoes had any fear of her vicious attack they made no complaint. And as she thumped the hoe deep into the black earth, for no practical gardening reason, she gradually worked her way out of her mental state, and was able to face the idea of a left-over supper with some equanimity. Even Becky, coming back in a gay mood, faced the baked ham with no complaints.

'You should see the house, Ma,' she said. 'You remember the Reed family left it in such a mess, and he's had it all restored. He even opened up the fireplaces—the ones that were bricked up for almost fifty years. And the furniture, Ma. Like you've never seen before. All wonderful! And Mattie has her own room up on the third floor. There's another big bedroom up there, too, and a bath. And on the second floor there's a great big bedroom, bigger than our living room, and it's got its own bath, too. And there are six more bedrooms, and a kitchen like you wouldn't believe, and——'

'All right. All right already. You don't have to describe his house. I agree it must be wonderful, but couldn't we change the subject?'

'Ma?' She looked up from her plate, where she had been pushing a slice of ham around among the mashed potatoes, trying to make it look as if she were eating. Becky was looking at her with her head cocked to one side, and those dark eyes were glimmering with suspicion.

'You're not sick or something?'

'Not even or something,' Mary said solemnly.

'Then you gotta be in love, Ma!'

'Why—wh—where did you get that silly idea,' she sputtered. 'That's a silly thing to say to your mother!'

'Come off it, Ma. I seen—I saw a movie last week about middle-aged love. It was great!'

'Middle-aged love? Why you impertinent child! I'm only twelve years older than you, and—and just where do you think you're going?'

'I promised Anna I'd come down tonight. Henry has a Grange meeting, and Anna said she could teach me how to crochet. And don't forget that Bruce is coming over tonight.'

'Bruce? You mean Mr Latimore? It doesn't pay to get familiar with your employers, Becky. I'm glad you're going to learn crocheting. And I'm so glad to see that you and Anna get along well. I—sort of have the feeling that maybe she doesn't like me.'

'She's scared of you, Ma. Every time Henry has something good to say, it's always about you. And you've never called on them, you know. They've been back from their honeymoon for two weeks, and you've never called.'

'Scared of me? Lordy, she must be eight inches taller than me, and twenty pounds heavier. What a silly notion!'

'And you're little Mrs Perfect, Ma. She's intimidated and you'd better believe it. She told me so. Why don't you go down and call on her?'

'Why—why I can't, my dear,' she tried to explain. 'It's an old New England custom. Just because they're back home doesn't mean that they've finished their honeymoon. It's the custom for mother-in-laws to wait for an invitation, which signifies that they're ready to face the world again.'

'Custom—smushton!' Becky snorted. 'So all right, it's the custom. I'll bet Anna never heard of it, or Henry either. I'll mention it in the conversation.'

'Casually, dear.'

'Yeah, sure, casually. You like Anna don't you?'

'Like her? My goodness, yes. She's just right for Henry. And now I only have to keep my eyes open for a man for you!' They both giggled, until Becky said, 'Oh no you don't, you're not going to get rid of me that quickly!' Mary pulled the girl closer, in a hug that spoke of more than affection. 'No,' she said, 'I've got no intention of getting rid of you that quickly, my dear. I'll want to keep you on hand until——'

'Until *I* can find a man for *you!*' Becky announced. 'Treat Bruce—Mr Latimore, kindly, Ma!' And with that she slipped out the door and sauntered down the path to Henry's house, still whistling.

Mary watched her from the window, holding back a corner of the chintz half-curtain until the girl dropped out of sight over the curl of the hill. When she dropped the curtain and turned back to the room she could not restrain her laughter. 'Why that little snip is not only planning to marry me off,' she snorted aloud, 'but she skipped out without helping with the dishes!'

After the kitchen clean-up Mary wandered upstairs, still in a kind of daze, to shower and shampoo her hair. She wandered back to her room dressed in her usual towel, and looked woefully at her closet's offerings. 'Discouraging,' she told herself. 'Just plain discouraging. I haven't bought a dress-up dress in four years. And I've got dirt under my fingernails. Why in the world didn't I want to plant flowers instead of potatoes? What a night this will be. I'll wear that blue blouse, and the plaid wrap-around skirt, and I'll make a corsage of potato-sprouts, with a stalk of celery in the middle? I'll play "Earth-Mother".' Which brought a sharp halt to the one-sided conversation. All the millions of statuettes coming out of the Middle East, she suddenly remembered, had shown that lovely lady as short, round, and very, very pregnant!

She had planned to be carefully dressed, in something cool and distant, lounging in the living room with her feet up, so to speak. So naturally, since it had been that kind of a day, she was still upstairs trying to braid her hair when the doorbell rang, and startled her back into real-time. She rushed for the stairs, halted when she happened to notice that she had neither blouse nor bra on, and retreated to correct at least half of that error. By the time she managed to get downstairs, hair still unbraided, blouse only half-buttoned, and skirt on almost sidewise, his heavy finger was not only demolishing the door bell, but he was pounding on the panel as well.

'I'm coming, I'm coming!' she yelled as she tugged

the skirt around to the front, managed another two buttons on the blouse, and gave up on her hair entirely. When she swung the door open he was leaning against the side of the house with one hand, laughing at her. She swallowed, and waved him in. As he walked by her one of his big hands patted her gently on the head.

'Why—why are you so much taller tonight?' she gasped, after searching mindlessly for something more germane to say.

'Not me,' he chuckled. 'You forgot those four-inch heels. Could we sit down? You look flustered.'

'Well, I—I guess I am,' she replied, her strain of honesty overwhelming her discouragement at being found in such a mess. And why do you care? The little voice inside her head niggled at her some more. Why do you care? Shut up, she roared back. Just plain shut up! She followed him into the living room, where he sank down on the couch. 'Something to refresh?' she offered tentatively. 'Coffee? Wine? Something stronger?'

'What I need,' he said, 'is a belt of something strong. Dutch courage is what I need.'

'I—I don't know that much about drinks,' she apologised. 'I don't have anything called Dutch Courage. I do have some six-year old sour mash. Sipping bourbon, my husband used to call it.'

'Yes. Just the thing,' he snorted. 'Something your husband recommended. On the rocks, please.'

He certainly didn't look pleased. The frown on his face was spreading wrinkles all across his cheeks and forehead. What have I done now, she asked herself. He looked perfectly happy when he came in. Did I say something wrong? Am I so much out of practice dealing with grown men?

She padded out to the refrigerator and dropped two ice cubes into each of two glasses. She filled her own with Coke, then went back to the bar in the living room, and filled his glass to the rim with Jack Daniels.

He snatched at it like a drowning man. She walked over to the chair opposite him, curled herself up with her feet under her, and offered a tentative toast before she sipped. His glass was already empty.

'I'm sorry,' she said, 'I didn't notice that you were so—so thirsty. Would you like another?'

'Yes. Stay where you are. I'll get it.'

She watched him walk over to the bar, refill his glass, and return to the couch. Neither said a word. He set the glass down on the coffee table, plonked himself down on the couch again, and stared over at her. As if daring me, she thought. As if daring me to—what?

'Your message said something about this being a personal visit, Mr Latimore,' she said softly. 'Personal?'

'Ah yes,' he returned. 'Personal. Meaning that it has nothing to do with the road.'

'Oh?' For her very life she could not think of a single better response. She managed another sip from the Coke glass in her hand, then set it down carefully on the end table, and folded her hands into her lap.

'Yes,' he repeated, 'personal, as in you and I.'

You and I, she thought, her mind twisting crazily back to her classes in English composition. You and I are the subject of the sentence. You and me are the object. I'm the subject of the visit? He's the object? We're both—oh lordy let my brain be clear this night!

'I've known you now for almost half a month,' he said, 'and every day I find out more about you.' He reached into his jacket pocket and whipped out a little note book. My God, she thought, he's not only been listening to gossip, he's been writing it all down!

'I'm not at all sure I appreciate this much attention,' she said primly.

'It's not been difficult,' he laughed. 'Everybody in town is more than willing to talk about the lovely widow Chase.'

'I'll bet they have,' she returned scornfully. 'That's one of the problems of life in a small village. But I wouldn't have thought that a man of your—er—stature would spend a deal of time listening to gossip. Especially about me. There seems to be no limit that you'll go to to get your road finished!'

He reached angrily for his glass and took a gulp that half-emptied it. 'I told you when I came in that this has nothing to do with the road. The damn road!' he roared at her.

She shivered back deeper into her chair. He hadn't come about the road. More than likely he had come to murder her or something! Here she was, all alone with this—this wonderful man, and—how in the world did that word slip in? How could such a wonderful man come all this way to murder her? The giggle broke out before she could control it.

'Okay, go ahead and laugh,' he retorted. 'Just because I'm out of practise with a homebody like you!'

'What in the world are you talking about?' she snapped. Homebody, indeed. As if she were a calico widow fresh off the wagon train! She smothered her impulse to hit him, smoothed her skirt, and tried again.

'All right, Mr Latimore,' she said. 'Perhaps I've started us out on the wrong foot. Shall we start again. You were saying that you've known me for half a month. And?'

'You really don't believe me, do you?' He was grinning again, so that, at least, was one good step forward. He waved his notebook at her from across the room. 'Listen to this,' he said, flipping to the first page.

'Mary Kate Flannigan, twenty-seven years old. You've lived all your life in Eastboro, most of it in this house. You came here with your mother when you were twelve years old. Your mother was Colonel Chase's housekeeper. His wife was sickly. She died in childbirth. Rebecca, I believe?'

'Yes,' she nodded distant agreement. 'Rebecca was an unplanned addition. Elizabeth was forty-two years old at the time.'

'And then you and your mother continued to live here until Becky was four years old, at which time your mother died. You remained here as housekeeper, and then the Colonel married you. You were seventeen years old, and he was fifty-one!' He pronounced the last sentence as if it had a bad taste, or was some deadly sin. She stared at him coldly, wondering what was coming next. He closed the notebook and watched her with narrowed eyes.

'It was a marriage of convenience, of course,' he said in a hard monotone. 'Everybody I meet says so. It would not have been proper for you to stay in the same house with him otherwise.' He was staring at her now, with a deep beetling look that seemed to beg for agreement.

'Which only shows you how wrong you can get, listening to gossip,' she told him coldly. 'For your information, the Colonel and I married for love. Do you suppose age has to be the grand arbiter of love?'

'Oh I could see that,' he agreed. 'You were close— propinquity and all that. I understand.'

'Do you? Do you really understand?' She got up from her chair and padded over in front of him. For years she had palmed off gossip-seekers who questioned her marriage. But now, for some reason, she wanted this man to understand, to know every detail of the story. 'We married for love,' she reiterated. 'That's the only reason I could ever marry. For love. And the Colonel and I were married, Mr Latimore. Husband and wife in every spiritual and physical sense of the word! The only regret I ever had was that I could never give him another child. Just before we were married he had to have an operation to remove his prostate gland. It made it impossible for him to be a father, but put no other limits on our—sex life. Now do you understand, Mr Latimore?'

He looked like a man who had just been kicked in the

stomach by an angry mule. She watched him for a second, then retreated to her chair. He grabbed up his glass and downed the other half of its contents. While he regained his composure she studied the flower motif in the worn rug at her feet. That's one of my troubles, she whispered to herself. I've surrounded myself with everything old—everything the Colonel wanted, everything he loved. And without him, what have I left of myself?

'Thank you for telling me,' he said formally. 'It makes me feel as if I know you a lot better. I appreciate that.'

'Well, you don't know me,' she said quietly. 'You know *about* me, but you don't know me. Aren't you going to write it down in your notebook?'

'Don't be silly, Mary Kate,' he returned. 'There's nothing written in this notebook, except for a first-page reminder. I'll show it to you in a minute. And don't think that I really don't know you. There's more in my mind than your first marriage. I know, for example, that you're a graduate of an agricultural college, and that you're still going to school.'

She shrugged that off. 'Common knowledge,' she said.

'I know that you have a warm heart, strong loyalties, and love deeply when you love. I also know that after you take a shower you paddle around the house topless, and that you never wear a bra unless you're going out to some important function. How's that?'

'How's that?' she gasped. 'Why you're nothing but a voyeur! A dirty old man! Where in the world did you——'

'Dirty middle-aged man,' he said, stopping her tirade in midstream. 'To be exact, I'm thirty-six years old, healthy, wealthy, and—well, we'd better leave that last part.'

'Becky,' she snapped. 'Becky and that daughter of yours. What are they trying to do to me?'

'As best I can tell,' he said softly, 'they're trying to get you married off. And I'm the prime candidate!'

'You! But——' She swallowed hard again. Her churning thoughts were altogether too revealing at this particular moment. 'Of course,' she said, 'it's a silly idea. Just because you settle in town—to get your road built of course—they are just—children daydream a lot, don't they?' Now it was her turn to plead for agreement, and not receive it. He dropped his notebook on the table, got up for a refill of his drink, and stood beside her chair. She found it impossible to look up at him.

'When you sit right down and analyse the situation,' he said, 'it's not as silly as it first appears. Mattie thinks you would make an ideal mother. Becky firmly believes that you're the finest woman in the world. Spending all your talents on one girl, when you could just as easily mother two, seems to be a waste. A terrible waste. Marriage is certainly indicated.' He walked by her and sat down on the couch again. She could not help but notice that his glass was already empty.

'On the other hand,' he ruminated, 'here I am, a man with many social requirements, needing a hostess very badly, and sick of the kind of woman I meet in my own circles around the world. And here you are. You're lovely to look at, skilled in the kitchen, a magnificent hostess, full of ambition, and all going to waste. Once again, marriage is indicated.'

She shook her head, trying to clear away the cobwebs. There he was, sitting on her couch, in her house, drinking her bourbon, and talking like a man who had lost at least half of his marbles! And yet he was a hard-headed business man. While he had been listening to gossip in Eastboro, she had spent some of her nights in Boston doing the same. Not only hard-headed, but also hard-hearted, the word in Bean City had been.

'I—I've never been the subject of a computer analysis,' she faltered. 'As far as I can see, marriage—our marriage—might be good for Mattie. You certainly don't know how to raise her. And it might be good for Becky, I acknowledge that. Becky's at the age where she needs a father-figure. And I can certainly see how you might profit by it. But don't you think—wouldn't you believe that perhaps I might want something from a marriage, too?'

'Why of course you do,' he returned. 'You want warmth and companionship, the security that wealth can bring, attention, company, new clothes. Have I missed anything?'

'Oh no,' she assured him through tight lips. 'You've hit every target—every target but me! You must be mad to come here with this—this discussion. What in the world are you thinking of? We're enemies, you and I. There's more trouble between us than there is friendship. Surely you can see that?'

He stood up and came over to her. His strong hands seized her wrists and pulled her up. One of his arms came around her, pressing her into the softness of his linen shirt, while the other fingered her loose hair. Then he dropped his hand to her chin, tilted it up, and kissed her. There were no bells ringing. No startling feelings running up and down her spine. There was just a warm, moist comfort about it, that released her taut nerves, and allowed her muscles to relax. She slumped against him, wiggling her arms around his broad waist, and letting the comfort flow into every tiny nucleus of her being. It felt like—coming home.

When he finally pushed her back into her chair she had totally surrendered to the perfection of peace which she had attained.

'So, now then,' his deep voice seemed to come from a million miles away. 'You don't really hate me, do you?'

'No. I—I don't hate you.'

'And you liked being kissed by me?'

'I—I liked it very much,' she admitted.

'Then that's the personal business I came over to talk to you about,' he said. 'I intend to marry you, Mrs Chase. Not right this minute. You're not ready for that. This is just my declaration, you understand. I'm going to marry you one of these days, when we both can get around to it.'

'And I'm not to have anything to say about it, Mr Latimore?' she asked softly.

'Not a great deal,' he returned. 'I don't intend to press you until I get you cornered, so that there's no escape.'

'That sounds pretty outrageous,' she said, trying to sound positive and decisive, but wishing in her heart that he would condescend to kiss her again. But instead of kissing her, he replaced his empty glass on the bar, and started for the door.

'So—so soon?' she managed to stammer.

'It's Mattie,' he explained over his shoulder. 'I have a babysitter, but only until ten. You know how that is. And, oh yes, there is one other thing. I've made my declaration, and I've kissed you. Don't you think perhaps you could now give up that Mr Latimore business, and call me Bruce?'

'I—yes—I—yes, Bruce,' she stuttered. He gave her a big smile and walked out to the front door. She followed behind him, a little numb from the conversation. He tapped her gently on the nose as he stood in the open door.

'Don't take it all so seriously,' he counselled her. 'There's a long time to go. The hunt's just begun!'

'But you haven't—you didn't——' she took a deep breath and pulled her shoulders back, military style. 'You didn't say anything about love,' she half-whispered.

'No. Of course I didn't,' he said bleakly, 'because we

both know you're still in love with the Colonel.' And then he was gone.

She wandered back to the living room and absent mindedly began to gather up the glasses. She wiped off the bar and the coffee table with a paper napkin, and carried the things out to the sink. Her Coke glass was still half-full. She made a face, and sent it down the drain. *Because you're still in love with the Colonel!* She leaned against the sink and looked out the window at the sweep of the stars. Orion the Hunter was moving southward from Polaris. Even the stars favour the hunter, she told herself bitterly. You're still in love with the Colonel!

Her mind made up, she dried her hands and stalked back into the living room, with an empty glass in her hand. She went directly to the bar, poured herself a generous portion of Courvoisier, and gulped it all down. She was still coughing as she moved over to the couch and sat down. Her mind was wrestling with a serious problem, one she had never grappled with before. You're still in love with the Colonel. She looked around the room with different eyes, then went back for another glass of cognac. An hour later she made her way slowly up to bed, and passed a troubled night, filled with dark dreams.

CHAPTER FIVE

MORNING brought a tired awakening, and a knowledge, not completely explored, that her life had taken a new turn. The house and its contents seemed to be flickering in and out of focus. But by the time Becky came down Mary had managed to paper over her troubles, and the girl was all agog to hear the report on the night's activities. Mary hardly knew what to say, but of course she had to say something. And so she compromised. 'Mr Latimore—Bruce—and I—we talked awhile, and—and we decided that we would try to establish a friendlier relationship, baby.'

'You mean you're going steady?'

'Well, perhaps not *that* friendly. I think we'll devote some time to each other, and perhaps cut down—slightly—on our involvement with—with others. You know what I mean?'

'I don't see how you could cut down,' her step-daughter said disgustedly. 'You haven't gone out with a man in the last five years, that I recall. Oh, you mean he will?'

'I really don't know, Becky. It wasn't all that—clear cut, you know. He didn't come right out and say—well, he didn't.' But he had, of course, and the little lie bothered her. She had always been honest and straightforward with Becky, and now, for a man, she was telling lies!

'Well, anyway. Did you make out?' Becky persisted.

'Make out? What in the world does that mean?'

'Oh, you know, Ma. Did you?'

'I don't know what you mean, young lady,' she snapped, mainly because she *did* know but wouldn't admit it. 'And I think that's enough conversation about that subject. How did you make out—I mean, how did you get on with Anna?'

'Oh I got on fine.' The girl was giggling at her! 'I told her about you visiting, and all, and she sent an invite. Tomorrow night, for supper, and please bring me and Mattie and Bruce, if he'll come. And Ma, she's scared to death. She can't cook the way you do, and her house is too small, and she's all up tight. She was almost crying when I left. What do you think?'

'What I think is that it's ridiculous. Do you suppose I knew how to cook before the Colonel took me in hand? Or keep house, or anything? What's the weatherman say for tomorrow?'

'Clear and hot is what the radio said.'

'So okay, she's got a fine patio down there, and the weather will be good, and how could you go wrong with a barbecue? Call her up, or sneak down there, or something, and give a hint. Right?'

'Ma, you *are* a wonder!' Becky threw her arms around her stepmother, then ran for the door. 'One hint, coming up!' she yelled.

Mary Kate stood at the foot of the stairs and shook her head. 'Well, perhaps I am,' she told herself sarcastically, and then headed back to the kitchen.

But the barbecue went well, and her course with her daughter-in-law was smoothed. But her relationship with Latimore became more and more involved. With school starting, a conflict in his schedule had arisen. He came down from his Boston offices at about five o'clock, but Mattie was out of school at three, and Becky at two-thirty. After a couple of false starts, they arranged for the little girl to take the number six school bus at the end of each day, and be delivered to the doorstep of the farm. There she played, wandered, and sometimes even studied, until her father came for her at five-thirty.

He took up the habit also, of dropping in unannounced; and once a week, on Wednesday, they formally dated. He took her to Boston, where they dined on lobster at Loue's On the Wharf. He also took her to Taunton, where they dined on Murphyburgers at a roadside stand. And at both ends of the spectrum they laughed at little jokes, held hands, and occasionally kissed. He was a sports-freak. He took her to the Raynham dog track, but she could tell one greyhound from another only when they wore their numbers. He took her to Shaefer Stadium to watch the New England Patriots squeak out a football victory over the Miami Dolphins, and all the way home he chided her for cheering for the wrong team.

They went to Boston once to hear the Symphony, and twice to see Swan Lake. And on the way home, after much nagging, she persuaded him to drive her through the Combat Zone. He checked twice to see that she had her window up, and the door locked before they went, and then had the nerve to tell her to shut up after she begged him to stop at one of the street corners so she could at least read the signs.

'Well how am I supposed to know?' she asked plaintively. 'They don't have any strip shows in Eastboro, or any—what was that—All Night Nudies, See Everything Before Your Eyes. What does that mean, anyway?'

'It means,' he started to say, and then clamped his jaw shut and made a big thing out of manoeuvring through lines of cars to get on to Route 128, the eight-lane highway that circles Boston. Which she didn't take too seriously, since there were only eight or ten cars visible on the entire freeway. 'What does it mean,' she insisted.

'And how in the world would I know,' he sighed. 'I don't go to places like that!'

'Such innocence,' she mused. 'Will you take me some night? There were lots of women there.'

'Don't be so double-damn silly,' he snapped. 'They're all working girls. No, I won't. Shut up, for God's sake. Do you have to be a nagger?'

He got even with her the night she took him to Providence to see a local production of Madame Butterfly. Not more than ten minutes into her favourite opera, when Butterfly first appeared before the Lieutenant, he took her hand in his and tugged her up out of her seat, and out of the theatre. She had barely time to catch her breath before they were standing under the marquee, watching a dismal fall rain drip slowly down on a somnolent city.

'Now what was that about,' she roared at him over the rain-noise. 'I like Madame Butterfly!'

'So do I,' he snarled back at her as he led her out into the rain towards the parking lot. He unlocked the car, thrust her into the seat like an unwanted package, and stomped around to the driver's side. She was so angry with him that she sat stiffly in place and refused to unlock his door for him. Which gave him another three minutes in the rain, fumbling with his keys. When he squished himself into the driver's seat he slammed the door, beat both hands on the steering wheel, and then looked at her with those predatory eyes.

'And just what was that all in favour of?' he snarled.

'You know!' she snarled back at him. 'I came to hear Butterfly, and you dragged me out without—what's the matter with you? I sat through your darned football game, didn't I? I love Madame Butterfly.'

'Yeah? Well I love Lt Pinkerton better. And how in the ever-loving world could you sit there and watch that loveable little guy try to make love to a two hundred pound Butterfly? If he had picked her up he would have had a double hernia!'

'Well she has to be big to contain that beautiful voice,' she protested.

'Yeah, sure,' he grunted, manoeuvring the big car

through the narrow streets of Providence Plantation. 'But opera's supposed to be a visual as well as an aural treat. And this one flunked out in the first act.'

'Spoil sport,' she grunted. 'You don't have any couth.'

'You'd better believe it,' he threatened. 'My family comes from a Scottish mill town. Button up. You want to stop for a burger?'

But nothing came of the argument. On their way home by way of Attleboro they saw an advertisement for professional wrestling. On the spur of the moment they stopped, and spent the rest of the evening laughing and cheering as the wrestlers rattled each other around the plywood-topped ring. After the last match, safely back in his car, she apologised very meekly. After all, two of the wrestlers had been smaller than Madame Butterfly, and as she remembered, it didn't hurt, now and again, to butter up the male ego.

On the 30th of September she got a very interesting telephone call from Charles Momson, just before lunch. It brightened things in every direction.

'They can't get back on the court calendar,' the lawyer told her gleefully. 'They came into the court this morning with the report on the wetlands, and Addie Blake, the court Clerk, told them that Judge Jaris had no open days until February 20th. So they left the brief with Addie, and a hearing date is tentatively set for the end of February.'

'But won't the Judge read the presentment, and maybe make an out-of-court ruling?' she asked.

'Oh come on with you, lass,' he laughed. 'I thought you were studying the law? Addie Blake and I went to school together. He won't even show that package to the Judge until February!'

'Then we're safe for the winter, Charley?'

'Safe as justice will allow, Mary Kate,' he returned; and then, after a pause, 'Well, providing he doesn't go back to the Great and General Court and have some of his buddies introduce a legislative bill.'

'Yes, I know,' she sighed.

'Now, now, Mary,' he said. 'Don't be bitter. The old adage says good lawyers work in the courts, mediocre ones run for office, and the terrible ones get jobs teaching at law schools. Right?'

She was too excited to hold it all in. Henry had been working at double time all month to get in the harvest, but the hay was hard to handle. The fields were at the far end of the farm, and the brook had to be crossed three times before the laden wagons could reach the barns. Besides, she needed an excuse, her relations with Anna had improved, but the girl still called her 'Mrs Chase', and fluttered around her like a five foot nine inch gypsy moth. What Mary needed was a valid excuse to visit her own step-son's house. An excuse. She automatically moved to her planning office, the kitchen. Her scheming room, Henry called it. She chuckled as she ran her fingers along the enamelled top of the gas stove, and then drew back from the heat. Of course! She whipped open the oven and looked at the two tiny but perfect lamb chops which were to be her lunch. Mary Chase, Mary the Perfect! She rubbed her itching nose, closed the oven door, and turned the thermostat up to 550 degrees. As she sprawled out on a kitchen chair to watch the proceedings, she shook her head sadly. 'What have you come to, Mary Chase,' she lectured herself aloud. 'Ever since that—that man came. First you learned to deceive, then you learned to lie, and now you're learning to connive. All in a good cause, of course. Aren't those some of the world's most famous last words?'

By now smoke was seeping out of the loose corner of the oven door. She found a hot pad, and looked in with satisfaction at the two blocks of carbon lying on the aluminium plate. Better be safe, she told herself.

Becky has too sharp an eye. She closed the door and let the chops burn for another five minutes. Then she shut off the oven and wandered upstairs to change from her light cotton dress to a pair of denims and a cotton shirt. She preferred dresses herself, but Anna was different—jeans would have to be the order of the day.

She took the chops out of the oven and set them on top of the stove, where Becky was sure to see them. Then she sauntered slowly down the hill to where Henry's house stood. Originally it had been the homestead of a separate farm, but when the Colonel had bought that farm for its acreage he had kept up the house for the time when Henry found a bride. And there she is, Mary Kate chuckled to herself. Five foot nine, one hundred and thirty pounds of Nordic splendour. Anna Michelson she had been before the wedding. Just Henry's size and speed. She came fluttering out of the house as soon as she caught sight of her mother-in-law.

'Is—was—something wrong?' the girl asked.

'Terribly wrong,' Mary admitted dolefully. 'Mary the magnificent has done it again.' She preceded the girl up on to the porch and dropped into the only available rocking chair.

'Done what?' Anna asked suspiciously. She was both surprised and perturbed, and probably would sooner have welcomed a visit from a rattlesnake than her mother-in-law. She had that tentative expression on her face, and kept looking over her shoulder as if hoping the Seventh Cavalry would ride up to her rescue.

'I burned my lunch,' Mary Kate told her. 'Again. Usually I just throw it in the garbage disposal, and get another something. But today I don't have a single thing unfrozen. Could I beg lunch from you, Anna?'

'You burned your lunch? I don't believe it! You didn't!'

'I'm afraid I did, Anna. As I often do. Do you really

believe all that nonsense of Henry's that I'm Mrs Perfect? There's no limit to what men will believe!'

The girl was laughing and crying at the same time. 'Yes, yes of course,' she managed between sobs. 'Of course. You burned your lunch—Ma?' The noun was tentative. She was trying it out for taste, for shape, having never used it before. Mary Kate smiled and rocked faster. 'Two lamb chops,' she confessed. 'Charcoal!'

'What a coincidence,' Anna laughed. 'That's just what we are having ourselves. Come along to the kitchen with me, and we'll have a look. Mary trailed her into the house, like a tugboat bobbing in the wake of the QE2. But her footsteps faltered as they went down the hall. She could smell smoke. And so could Anna.

When Henry came up from the barns for lunch he found the two of them talking ten to the minute over the dining room table, where individual crab-salad plates awaited the diners. He washed noisily in the kitchen, and came through.

'Crab—salad?' he asked dubiously.

'Of course,' Mary assured him. 'It's my first lunch in your home, and your wife knew that crab-salad was my favourite lunch!'

'Why of course,' he muttered, looking at her out of the corner of his eye. To the best of his knowledge Mary had never eaten crab salad willingly in all the days of her life! 'There's a funny smell in the kitchen,' he added.

'It's a new kitchen cleaner,' his wife told him. 'Ma brought it down for me to try out.'

Henry only *looked* slow, beneath his heavy forehead was a first class brain. He heard not only the words, but also the subtle toning of the conversation. 'Well, in that case you're all right,' he commented. 'Ma's perfect. She never makes mistakes.'

'Ain't it true,' his wife laughed, but Mary kept a

sober face, and took the opportunity to tell him of their reprieve.

'That's a good thing,' he commented when she had finished her explanation. 'Now we can relax a little. We still have hay, and those Guyana Hybrids could stand a few days more. So we should be free of that worry for the winter.'

'Yes, I think so,' Mary replied. 'But please don't think that the fight is over, I can almost see it in his eyes that he means to build that road. By spring we'd better all be battened down and ready for a blow!'

But September faded into October, and the hills turned from green to scarlet and gold. November blew in, cold and wet, and only pumpkins stood in the fields among the abandoned corn stalks, and nothing really had changed. Nothing important, that is. True, she had become accustomed to Wednesday nights with Bruce, and during the second week of November when he didn't show up, she sat by the telephone quite forlornly. When it did ring he was calling from Boston where an emergency meeting had been called because of a disaster in Colombia. She said all the right quiet words, but when he hung up, she cried.

There was something else that she began to notice. When she was in a room, alone or with a crowd, whenever he came in she would know it without seeing him. It was as if his entrance brought a calming effect with it; as if a little vacant spot in her heart had been properly filled. And when he went away the emptiness returned. She would start to snap at people, moon over her coffee, sigh for—what else, his return. Just that, nothing more. It wasn't necessary that he touch her, or speak, or draw attention. All he had to do was to be there. Very companionable, she told herself when she had reasoned it all out. Very friendly. We've become good friends. But in the back of her mind was that niggling concern, because she knew that whatever it was in this web he was spinning, it wasn't meant to be friendship. And the thought chilled her.

Thanksgiving, at the end of November, was a great success. They all met at the main farm house, Anna and Henry, Becky with a young man named Alfred in tow, Mattie, Bruce, and Mary Kate. It made for a festive occasion. Anna and Becky joined Mary in the kitchen early, to watch the turkey gradually brown, prepare the vegetables, and guard the pies from random male raids. They ate at four o'clock. When they sat down only the turkey was stuffed, when they rose for coffee everyone *but* the turkey was. The men all congregated in the living room to watch the last quarter of the Notre Dame football game. The women cleared the monstrous pile of dishes, stacked the dishwasher, and sat down to digest their meal and to gossip. About ten minutes into their gossip session Bruce wandered in from the living room, and put his arm on her shoulder. When she looked up at him, smiling, everyone in the room except herself noticed what a special smile it had become.

'We'll take a walk,' he ordered gently. 'Leave the dishes with the kids.'

She got up wordlessly, accustomed now, after months of practise, to following where he led. He helped her into her sheepskin coat, and settled himself into his bulky driving coat. They went out the front door and down the pebbled walk to the massive stump of the Liberty Tree. Indian Summer had faded away, the sun had set by six o'clock, and low in the sky they could see the cold round disc of the Hunter's Moon. Without thought they climbed up on to the massive stump and sat with their arms around each other. In the distance they could hear the high call of the hunting owl. A vagrant wind tousled the tendrils of hair which had escaped her knitted wool pullover cap. The trees around them were bare sticks. She nestled her head against his warm shoulder.

'The Liberty Tree,' he prompted.

'What?'

'The Liberty Tree. You were going to tell me about it.'

'Oh, that.' It took a moment for her to bring her mind back to the subject. It had been wandering in a most unseemly manner, aided considerably by the strength of his arm, and the entirely male smell of him. She struggled slightly away from him so she could concentrate.

'Every town had one,' she lectured primly. 'Before the Revolution, that is; always a big tree that could shelter a meeting. The colonists established Committees of Correspondence. Men in each town who wrote the Revolutionary news to specific men in other towns. By the King's mail, of course, King George could have wiped out the revolution by closing his post offices. Well, the local men would meet under the Liberty Tree, hear the latest news, and make their plans; and so the Liberty Tree became the core of the American Revolution!'

'In the cold of winter? Why the heck didn't they hire a hall?'

She looked up at him in surprise. 'You'd make a lousy conspirator, Bruce,' she told him. 'The tree was always isolated in some place where nobody could sneak up on you and hear what was going on!'

'And of course your family had a big part in all this?' He was grinning again, and she almost felt like hitting him.

'Of course not,' she snapped. 'My family didn't come over from Ireland until 1861. Just in time for my great grandfather to be drafted into the Union Army in the Civil War. But the Colonel's family—well, I guess you know that the Chases came over on the Mayflower!'

'Must have been one hell of a big boat,' he snapped back at her.

They sat quietly until his stern face gradually relaxed, and then he turned her towards him and kissed her gently. It was what she had become accustomed to, a warm friendly kiss that just felt good. And then for a moment his grip tightened. The pressure of his lips demanded something more, but what more she could not say. When she failed to respond he released her, and laughed.

'What's that in honour of?' she asked. His laugh bothered her more than the kiss did. She was becoming too sensitive to his moods, she scolded herself.

'Just testing,' he retorted. 'Every now and again when you're making a stew you have to taste it to see if the seasoning is proper. Not so?'

'I suppose,' she sighed. 'If only I knew what you were talking about. Look over there. Shooting stars! Just below Cassiopea. See it?'

'Yes,' he replied, 'Did you make a wish?'

'Don't be silly,' she teased him. 'That's starlight starbright, first star I've seen tonight—you don't wish on meteor showers.'

'I do,' he whispered in her ear as he pulled her closer. 'I wish on every damn thing I can find!' She nestled against him again, until the chill of the night began to seep through their clothes. They walked back up the hill, without words, to where the lighted windows of the old farmhouse beckoned them.

But Christmas was when the world came apart at the seams. The week before the holiday, on a bitter-cold Saturday morning, he came to take her to the coast. It was so cold outside that she hardly knew whether to take him seriously, and his casual attitude irritated her. She put on her warmest boots and socks, her thickest trousers, two sweaters, and a heavy hooded coat. He drove her the thirty miles to Plymouth, the old town where the Mayflower had landed the first settlers, but now more renowned for its accident-prone nuclear power plant. The thermometer outside hovered around the ten degree Fahrenheit mark.

He pulled her out of the car and tugged her at speed through a quick tour of the *Plymouth Plantation*, the reconstruction of the original Pilgrim village. It consisted of several log cabins, surrounded by a wooden pale to keep the Indians at bay. Only a couple of the actors hired to impersonate the early Pilgrims were on the street, and only one ticket collector was available as they struggled to the wharf, where a full-scale replica of the Mayflower lay open to inspection.

'I'm freezing,' she complained, to no avail. But she did break her hand loose from his when he swung himself up into the rigging and taunted her to follow. 'It's not such a big ship after all,' he yelled down to her, 'considering it would have to carry ten thousand people, if you believe the genealogists!'

'I wish I knew what you're trying to prove,' she muttered as he rejoined her on the deck. She had managed to warm her hands by shoving them down into the waistband of her trousers, but the tips of her ears were feeling the bite of the frost.

'Prove?' he laughed. 'What do I have to prove?' And at once he dragged her away from the Plantation and up the road to where a tiny, open Greek temple provided a granite shelter over the Plymouth Rock, the stepping-stone by which the Pilgrims had debarked from their shallop on to the new continent. 'It's a long way from the water now,' she noted. 'Did they move it when they put up this—this stupid cover.'

'No,' he returned. 'This is where the rock belongs. It's the sea that's moved away. Boy is it cold!'

'Well finally you got the message,' she sighed.

He grabbed her arm and propelled her at speed across the street and down the road to the Plymouth Inn. The welcome warmth hit her squarely in the face, bringing on a lassitude for which she was not prepared.

He urged her along to a table by the front window, and they sat quietly over hot black coffee. She could feel the numbness withdrawing from her toes, and a tingle of pain as the circulation returned to her earlobes. 'Bruce——' she started to say, just as he spoke too. She waited.

'Mary Kate,' he said, 'I wanted you to come so I could talk to you without all that crowd that hangs around you.'

'Don't talk like that,' she laughed. 'One of them is yours, remember?'

'Do I ever remember,' he sighed. 'She's giving me a hard time at home, I'll tell you.'

'A hard time? She's never been nicer at the farm.'

'Well, that's because the farm's got something she wants. Namely you. And I want you too, Mary. Have you decided yet to fall in love with me?'

Her irritation at the temperature, the hour, his casual treatment of her, all welled up at once. 'Why that's a silly thing to talk about. I can't think of a less romantic place than this to talk about falling in love,' she snapped. 'Is that what you got me up so early for? It must be almost zero outside, and you want to talk about love?'

He frowned at her, his heavy eyebrows forming a straight line above his cold eyes. 'I take it then that the answer is no?'

She put a gloved hand on his arm. 'Bruce,' she pleaded, 'I don't know what the answer is. With the Colonel and me it was different. We knew each other well, and we lived in the same house, and it—it just happened.'

'Damn it, woman!' He got up in fiery anger, kicking his chair back into a corner of the room. 'I don't mind too much if you refuse me, but do you have to keep bringing the Colonel into our discussions? How the hell can I ever get you to love me when you cart the memorial of your dead husband around on your back all the time!'

'My God!' She stood up to face him, aflame with indignation. 'Don't you—don't you ever talk about the Colonel like that again! He was a gentleman!'

'Yeah,' he snarled, 'by Act of Congress. Come on, let's get out of here!'

They drove back to Eastboro in a different kind of silence, a seething resentful quiet. When he delivered her to her door she had the feeling in the pit of her stomach that this would be goodbye. And she was no more ready for that than she was for an open declaration of love.

'Would you and Mattie come for Christmas?' she asked.

'No,' he snarled. 'I'll be in Saudi Arabia, and Mattie is going to her grandmother's house in Newport.'

'So there—there doesn't seem to be anything more to say?'

'No. Goodbye, Mary Kate. God keep you.'

'And you, Bruce,' she returned. She slipped quickly out of the car, walked around to the driver's side, and leaned in through the open window. He kept his angry face straight ahead. With a sigh she kissed him on his cheek. As she pulled her head out of the car he gunned the engine and roared down the drive. The noise of the engine blotted out her final words: 'God keep you safe, my love,' she sighed on the wind. But it was too late.

The next morning both he and Mattie had disappeared. 'House is all locked up tight, Ma,' Becky reported. 'Mrs Pemm, who was his housekeeper, says he gave them all a month's pay and said he would let them know when he needed them again. And I hear by the grapevine that they had to carry Mattie out to the car, kicking and screaming up a storm!'

'Poor tyke,' Mary Kate sighed, trying to hold back the tears. If only no one else knew, she could salvage her own pride. But a poor little thing like Mattie, torn between two worlds, how could you explain life to Mattie?

The weather conformed to her mood. Christmas Day fell on a Friday, and the Monday before, a massive storm moved in all along the east coast. By Monday noon the clouds over Eastboro had blotted out the sun, on Tuesday the clouds spat a few flakes of snow at the town, and on Wednesday it began to come down in blizzard proportion. Henry came by, worried.

'Weather forecast's mean, Ma,' he said. 'I've got everything tied down. Becky's chicks are all locked in, but I'm worried about you, up here on the hill alone. Becky's coming to us tonight for the carol rehearsals, and she'll stay until Saturday. Why don't you come down with us?'

'No, I can't, Henry,' she returned. 'If I had my druthers, I'd druther be here alone. I've plenty of fuel and water, and the telephone. What else could I need.' A call on that damn telephone was what she needed, she knew, but she wasn't about to win the Stupidity Crown of the Year by telling Henry that she had to stay up here alone because—perhaps—Bruce might call!

'I don't know, Ma,' he said tenderly, 'but we don't want to risk you for anything. Tell you what I'll do. I'm going to bring my new tractor up here and park it by the house. The one with the tank treads on it. Those tracks will run through anything, and there's a heater in the cab. So if you get desperate, you turn on the key and come down the hill. You hear?'

'I hear,' she laughed. 'You sound more like your father every day.'

'Yeah well,' he laughed back as he ruffled her hair, 'you sound more like my mother every day, too. Goodnight, sweet.'

'Goodnight, son,' she said.

He turned back at the door, neglectful of the rising

winds and the spurts of snow. 'Those are the nicest words I could hear,' he told her. 'It's the best Christmas present I could have.' And he was gone into the snow.

The wind began to rise about seven o'clock that evening, howling around the exposed farmhouse like banshees. The house rocked, but suffered no damage. After Henry had positioned the tractor he had also closed the heavy wooden shutters on the house. Except for the four in the living room. She had refused at that point, not wanting to be completely enclosed by darkness. With the porch lights on she could see a little of the surrounding world. Heating might be a problem, she knew, so she went through the whole house checking radiators. She opened one hot and one cold water faucet in the bathroom just slightly, so that their constant drip would help keep the pipes from freezing.

By ten o'clock the house was the centre of a full-blown blizzard. She cuddled herself up in extra blankets and sat on the living room couch, listening to the radio. Television had failed her. The antenna had already blown off the roof. She dialled Henry's house, just to be sure that she was not alone in the world, and was gratified by the laughter in the background. At least somebody's happy, she told herself. And then she leaned back and gave full rein to her miseries. Where would he be now? Deep in the desert playing at Valentino and the Desert Song? Did he have a single thought for the tiny corn-haired woman he had left behind? Or did he even think about his road? She missed the warmth of him, the comfort, the trust, the support, the—the love of him. 'Oh God,' she prayed desperately, 'let him come back to me!'

She shook herself out of her daze, and walked out into the kitchen. A hot cup of chocolate might not save her soul but it could do something for her aching body. As she took her warm mug back into the living room the telephone rang. It was not a full solid ring, but a staccato series of interrupted sounds. Her first thought was for the children below the hill. She brushed aside the curtains at the window but could see nothing. The wind had dropped slightly, but the snow was falling in huge moist flakes. The phone jangled again. She walked over, put her chocolate down carefully, and picked up the instrument.

'Hello?' she answered cautiously. There was a whining on the wire, an open hum, as if the caller were a long, long way off. In the background she could barely hear a young voice.

'Hello, Ma?' the voice repeated. 'Help me, Ma. I need you.'

'Who—where are you,' she asked.

'It's me, Mattie,' the little voice responded. 'I'm stuck, Ma. I run away. I'm in the bus station at Taunton and everybody's gone home, and there ain't no more buses, and it's so cold, Ma. Help me?' And the line went dead.

For just a moment Mary Kate panicked, and then she settled down. She knew the bus station. No heat, wind-driven, cold, and eight miles away. Eight country road miles away. The best bet would be to call the police at Taunton. She picked up the phone. There was no dial tone. There was only one thing left to do. She rushed upstairs, changed into her thermal underwear, and all the heavy clothing she could find. Then back to the kitchen for a thermos of hot chocolate. Now, battle against the front door, being held closed by the wind, until she was able to squeeze out of the opening. Directly in front of her was the tractor, looking like a little yellow tank with a glass booth where the gun ought to be. The wind whipped at her as she struggled into the cab. She caught her breath, then fumbled with the key. The gasoline pre-starter kicked in, followed in minutes by the rumble of the big diesel engine. She watched closely as the panel instruments climbed up to full power. When she flashed on the lights and the windshield wipers she automatically shifted into forward speed and the heavy machine rumbled down the hill, scattering the two feet of snow which had accumulated. At the foot of the hill she stopped. The smartest thing to do would be go to Henry. Take Henry away from his family on this vicious night? All she had to do was to turn right.

She thought about it for a moment, just long enough for the heat to come up in the cabin. And her decision was taken. She pulled back the gear lever and turned left, on to the highway.

The wind howled at her as she moved out on to Route 138, going south. Twice she had to stop and wipe off the windshield, where the wet snow was already building up a bridgehead. But through all the wind and snow the heavy tractor clanked along at a steady eight miles an hour, up the hill at Sullivan's Ledge, through the two deserted blocks of downtown Eastboro, and out the other side. Occasionally a light could be seen, set back from the road, but nothing else moved except the wind and the tractor.

Once through they town they turned south west, into the teeth of the wind. The snow had already covered the road, obliterating the shoulders. She gave silent thanks to the engineers who had long since devised a cure. On each side of the road, set at intervals of one hundred feet, metal rods faced with reflectors marked the roadway. She stopped long enough to focus the tractor's two searchlights on the line of reflectors, and started off. The miles between Eastboro and Taunton were like a photo-montage of the end of the world. The long line of oak and maple that lined the road was bent northward by the force of the wind. Drifts were piling up on the east side of the road, driven by the insane fury of the wind. Eight miles an hour, the tractor clanked. It would take an entire hour to get there. And

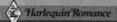
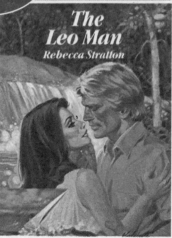

LOVE BEYOND REASON
There was a surprise in store for Amy!

Amy had thought nothing could be as perfect as the days she had shared with Vic Hoyt in New York City—before he took off for his Peace Corps assignment in Kenya.

Impulsively, Amy decided to follow. She was shocked to find Vic established in his new life...and interested in a new girl friend.

Amy faced a choice: be smart and go home...or stay and fight for the only man she would ever love.

MAN OF POWER
Sara took her role seriously

Although Sara had already planned her esc from the subservient posit in which her father's death had placed her, Morgan Haldane's timely appearc had definitely made it ea

All Morgan had asked in return was that she pose a fiancée. He'd confessed t needing protection from partner's wife, Louise, and part of Sara's job proved e

But unfortunately for heart, Morgan had told her about Monique...

Your Romantic Adventure Starts Here.

THE LEO MAN
"He's every bit as sexy as his father!"

Her grandmother thought that description would appeal to Rowan, but Rowan was determined to avoid any friendship with the arrogant James Fraser.

Aboard his luxury yacht, that wasn't easy. When they were all shipwrecked on a tropical island, it proved impossible.

And besides, if it weren't for James, none of them would be alive. Rowan was confused. Was it merely gratitude that she now felt for this strong and rugged man?

THE WINDS OF WINTER
She'd had so much— now she had noth

Anne didn't dwell on it, bu the pain was still with her— double-edged pain of gri and rejection.

It had greatly altered her; Anne barely resembled th girl who four years earlier left her husband, David. H probably wouldn't even recognize her—especially with another name.

Anne made up her mind. just had to go to his house discover if what she suspec was true...

These FOUR free Harlequin Romance novels allow you to enter the world of romance, love and desire. As a member of the Harlequin Home Subscription Plan, you can continue to experience all the moods of love. You'll be inspired by moments so real...so moving...you won't want them to end. So start your own Harlequin Romance adventure by returning the reply card below. <u>DO IT TODAY!</u>

BUSINESS REPLY CARD

First Class   Permit No. 70   Tempe, AZ

POSTAGE WILL BE PAID BY ADDRESSEE

**Harlequin Reader Service
2504 W. Southern Avenue,
Tempe, Arizona 85282**

NO POSTAGE
NECESSARY
IF MAILED
IN THE
UNITED STATES

for the first time, fear struck at her. What if the tractor stopped? What if the fuel ran out? Hurriedly she checked the fuel gauge. It read half-empty. How much did the tank hold? Thirty gallons? So she had fifteen gallons left. One gallon to the mile, that had always been Henry's estimate. One gallon to the mile. The perspiration ran down her face as she fumbled with the simple arithmetic. But before she had computed an answer the road began to rise, turned right, and she was clanking down the streets of Taunton, at the Town Green. And there would be enough fuel to get back!

The wind, offset by the massive courthouse buildings on the Green, dropped to a purr. Even here, in the centre of the city, there was not another track in the snow, save hers. Nothing stirred. The streetlights were out, and drifts of snow, as high as eight feet, were accumulating in the lee of the buildings. She stopped once more to wipe off the windshield, then clanked down Court Street towards the bus terminal. As she pulled alongside the old wooden building she idled the diesel, shifted into neutral on both tracks, and looked anxiously at the terminal.

It was a single storey structure, with offices on one side, and a tiny waiting room on the other. One small light gleamed in the waiting room, but she could see nothing. Perhaps the Police had come and taken her away? Maybe. But just down one building and across the street she could see the back parking lot of the Police station. And nothing moved in that direction. She looked up and down the street. There were no tracks in the virgin snow. The four buses in the adjacent parking lot looked like huddled mastadons, congregating to keep warm.

Weary from the tension of driving, she bundled herself up and slipped out of the cab. The wind snatched the plexiglass door out of her hands. It took all her strength to recapture it and close it behind her.

When she jumped off the tracks her feet buried themselves in snow. Bent over almost into a U, she staggered across to the door of the terminal. It was stuck. Futilely she beat against it with her tiny fists. The wind rose again, whistling down Court Street. The Montreal Express, she told herself. Straight out of Canada. Almost in despair she leaned her full weight against the door and bounced it with her ample hip. The door complained, quivered, and fell open. She staggered inside.

There was a little heat in the building, but just the absence of the wind made it feel like a furnace inside. She cleared her face of the snow that had adhered to her eyebrows, and looked around. No one. All four of the benches were empty. 'Oh Lord, where can she be?' she exclaimed to the empty building. And a tiny voice from under one of the video arcade games called, 'Here I am, Ma! Here!'

'Mattie!' she screamed, dropping to her knees to peer under the machine. 'Mattie?'

The little eyes stared back at her, wide open. The muffler around her face slipped just enough to show a smile. 'Hi Ma,' the little girl said. 'I knew you would come. Are you mad at me?'

She scooped the little body up in her arms and hugged it close to her. 'Mad at you?' she answered, fighting hard to hold back the tears. 'After you came all this way to spend Christmas with me? C'mon, kid, let's go home.'

CHAPTER SIX

IN the end they all spent Christmas at the big house.
The snow continued through Thursday morning, ending
just after noon. Mattie and Becky shared a room, while
Henry and Anna made do with the old corner
room which had been neglected since the Colonel's
death.

'I still can't get over it, Ma,' Henry insisted. 'Why
would you do such an idiotic thing as to drive all the way
to Taunton by yourself. Why didn't you come for me?'

'I don't really know, dear,' she answered softly. 'I
thought—well, I thought it was for the best.'

'And you wore yourself out. And then, instead of
finding some place in Taunton to stay, you drove all the
way back! Ma, that's not like you.'

'Why it is too,' she retorted with considerably more
spirit. 'I didn't know a soul in Taunton, and not even
the police were on the streets. So I drove back to
Dr Gedde's house, which is halfway between Taunton
and here. I had to get Mattie to the doctor. And then
when he said she was okay—just needing bed and
breakfast—what else could be better than to drive the
other four miles home? I think I was very sensible!'

'Ma!' he sighed. 'It was the worst blizzard in seventy
years! You've got to stop thinking of yourself as
Goliath, you know. In fact, you hardly fit the
description of little David!'

'Well a lot you know!' she snorted. Which was the
best *non sequitur* she could think of. Just to emphasise
her mood, she flounced out to the kitchen, where Anna
and Becky were rolling dough for pie crusts. 'Men!' she
thundered at the two girls.

'I agree!' Anna returned. 'What's Henry done now?'

'Why ever men think they have all the best answers in the world, I'll never know,' Mary stated firmly. 'Especially considering what a terrible mess they've made of things! Your husband is turning into an arrogant male chauvinist, Anna. You must do something about him.'

'Oh I will,' Anna assured her solemnly. But Becky spoiled the scene by giggling, and it took only another minute for the other two to join in.

Mary Kate checked the clock, filled a mug with hot soup, and went up to the second floor. Mattie was awake, but lying very still in the centre of one of the two twin beds. She hunched herself up when she saw who was coming in the door. Mary Kate walked over slowly, to avoid spilling the soup, and set it down on the bedside table. She borrowed another pillow from Becky's bed, and propped the girl up in a sitting position.

'It has finally stopped snowing,' she told the girl. 'Here now, another sip of this soup. It's hot.' The girl smiled up at her and cuddled the warm mug between her hands.

'I just thought I'd never get warm,' she said. 'Gee it was so cold!'

'It wasn't the best time of the year to run away,' Mary commented. 'You want to tell me about it?'

'No. If I do, you'll be mad at me, and send me back.'

Mary pulled up a chair beside the bed, and dropped one hand on the little girl's arm. 'Hey now,' she said, 'You know me better than that. Besides, how could I send you anywhere? There's three feet of flat snow out there, and drifts up to seven feet. They're just ploughing out the County Road now, and I think they're working on the telephones. You're stranded here. So start talking!' She did her best Bogart imitation, which wasn't too good. But it was good enough to bring a smidgin of a smile to Mattie's eyes.

'Okay, okay,' she chuckled, and then her face grew sober again. 'Ma,' she said, 'They don't like me. Only Daddy likes me. And you.' She passed her empty cup back, and dropped her hands into her lap. 'Grandmother is a great lady. She likes to dress up and go to her friends. And they sit around and play cards, and say mean things about people. She made me go with her. Every day. Get a clean dress, Mathilda. Don't spill that, Mathilda. Sit quietly in the corner while grandmother talks to the ladies, Mathilda. Yuck! And the same thing at home. You're too young to eat with the family, my dear. Did you polish your shoes, Mathilda? You know something, Ma? They said I was too dumb to be in their school. And then I heard them.'

'You heard them what, Mattie?'

'They was all sitting in the living room, and I was thirsty, so I sneaked downstairs, and when I went by the door they were talking about Daddy. You know, he provided all the money they live on. And they were laughing, and calling him a barbarian—did I say that right? They was laughing at him. That's when I decided to come back to you, Ma. I hate them.'

'Well,' Mary said, stalling. What to make out of this mess. A grandmother in Newport whom she hated. A father in Saudi Arabia, whom she loved. Mattie would just have to stay in Eastboro. At least until someone could get in touch with her father. But there had to be something more. 'Well, little bit,' she told the child, 'You duck down under the covers and get some more sleep. You'll just have to stay with us, won't you? Until I can get in touch with your father, of course. Right?'

'Yes, Ma,' the little girl sighed. She slipped her thin body down in the bed, and held out her hand. 'But it would be ever so much easier if you would marry my dad.'

Mary stroked the hand and arm until the heavy eyelids closed, then tucked the arm under the covers.

'Perhaps you're right, darling,' she whispered as she walked quietly out of the room.

Henry was in the living room when she came down, with the telephone in his hand. He was talking to somebody.

'Is it fixed,' she asked inanely.

'No,' Henry laughed, 'I was just practising. I was talking to the sheriff's office. He says they're ploughing Main Street now, and hope to have the highway clear in two or three days. Nobody hurt. Evidently everybody—well, most everybody, had the sense to stay home.'

'Don't be a smart aleck,' she sighed. 'I've got to let her grandmother know, and then I've got to—to find her father, I guess. I don't even know her grandmother's name, and she won't tell me. She's afraid we'll send her back.'

'Of course. We'll have to, Ma. When everything's cleared up, we'll have to send her back.'

She turned on him and sputtered, her eyes gleaming. 'No such thing, Henry Chase! We'll not send her back. If that fool of a father of hers wants her to go back to Newport he can come and take her by himself. We're not sending her anywhere! Not anywhere. You hear me?'

'Hey Ma.' He put his hands on her shoulders, gently. 'No need to get into such a fuss as that. You're the boss. If you want her to stay, she stays.'

'Oh Henry!' She fell against him, sobbing. 'I just don't know what to do anymore. I'm so mixed up!'

He held her until the storm had passed, then used his big handkerchief to dry her eyes. 'It'll all turn out right, you'll see,' he said quietly. 'And as for the grandmother, they're snowed in down in Newport as badly as we are. So I'll just call the Newport Police and tell them that Mattie Latimore is safe with us. That *is* what's worrying you, isn't it?'

The little lie was almost out of her mouth when she

stopped it. She looked up at her towering step-son and managed a one-sided smile. 'No, Henry,' she said, 'That's not it.'

Unable to explain herself, she ran for the protection of the kitchen. Bread was what she needed. She pulled down the flour container while the two younger women watched in astonishment. Bread was what she needed. You mix the flour and the milk and the water and the other ingredients, and then you pound it and stretch it and smash at it and beat on it until all your frustrations are released. And the silly dough just lays there, and never tells the world what you are really up to!

They had a light supper. Henry carried Mattie downstairs, and they settled her, well-wrapped in the big arm-chair. They all ate soup, a strong hearty chicken and rice bowl, and afterwards it was time to decorate the tree. The snow had started again. Huge wet flakes, but with no wind.

There was no shortage of help, so Mary watched them for a minute, and then went back into the living room. She needed to think.

She threw herself down on the couch, curled her feet up under her, and let her mind roam. Suppose—just suppose—that he was serious, and would ask her a second time? Or was it true, what he had said, that she was for ever carrying the Colonel around on her back? She looked around the room, the solid dependable, protective room. Was that what it was? A protective room? She had wrapped herself up in the lives of Henry and Becky, no doubt. And through all the past years she had never looked further forward than Becky's wedding day. When Becky walked down the aisle with some lucky man, and went off to her own future, what would happen to Mary Chase? Could she bear it, the empty house, the visits from other people's children, the lonely vigils in a celibate bed? They all thought of her as a calm settled woman. Only she and the Colonel knew better. What would the Colonel say? She knew without asking. It was his favourite saying: 'Never look backwards. It's tomorrow that counts.'

The dear Colonel. She let memories flit through her mind, of all the happy times, the shared joys and troubles, the love that had filled the house. She toyed with each memory, turning it from side to side, as if it were a jewel of great price. And then, without regret, she placed them all in a treasure chest in her mind, and snapped the lock shut. Five years after his funeral the Colonel was finally laid to rest.

She tried to stand up. Her left foot was asleep. She stamped on it, listening with one ear to the laughter from the dining room. Somebody had to tell Bruce. Tell him what? Tell him that Mattie was safe, of course, you blithering idiot! Tell him too that—she shied away from the second idea. It wasn't time yet. A girl had to wait to be asked. And there was Becky to think of, too. With toes still tingling, she inched her way across to the telephone. The clock on the wall had stopped. Two hours till Christmas? She shrugged her shoulders and looked in her booklet for his office number in Boston.

The telephone seemed to ring for hours, and she was about to give up, when she heard a couple of snaps on the line and a grumpy male voice answered.

'Latimore Corporation, Emergency room.' He wasn't very pleased at being disturbed. She could hear all the vibrations of the irritated male ego ringing down the wire at her, and it sapped her courage. 'I'm—I—I need to talk to Mr Latimore,' she said, not too bravely.

'For God's sake, lady,' he roared. 'It's Christmas Eve. Don't you have a man of your own? He's not here.'

'But I have a problem,' she insisted.

'So do I,' he roared back. 'We've got seventy-five pieces of equipment scattered over half of New England, and the governor has just requisitioned them to clear the highways.'

It was too much for her. She was angry enough with Latimore the Roadbuilder, without having problems with Imperial Latimore, hiding away in his desert oasis! And then to have this loud-mouthed chauvinist talk down at her was just too much. And when a six-foot temper is concealed in a five-foot girl, it comes out with a rush.

'Now you listen here, you self-satisfied prig,' she roared back at him. 'I don't care if you've lost *all* your little toys in the snow. Poor boy. The governor is down in Florida for his vacation. So now sit up and listen. I've got a problem. I've got a little lost girl, and her name is Mattie Latimore! Now what have you got to say?'

'Holy murder!' he said, at considerably less volume than before. 'You mean the boss's kid?'

'Of course I mean the boss's kid—I mean, daughter.'

There was a pause, and she could hear him have some sort of background conversation with someone else. Then he came back to the phone.

'Lady, do you know where the child is now?'

'Yes, she's with me.'

'Er—lady, please don't tell me your name is Mary Chase?' The bear had become a koala in just a matter of minutes! She couldn't help but feel some elation. At least she had subdued *one* male ego. But she held the thought for only a second. After all, it wasn't *his* fault.

'Well,' she said pleasantly, 'if it means all that to you, I'd be glad to tell you that my name is not Mary Chase.' The sigh that came down the wire indicated he had been holding his breath. 'But unfortunately, it is.'

'Oh lady!' he muttered.

'I know,' she laughed, 'but you asked me not to tell you. What difference does it make?'

'What difference? I've been working for Latimore for thirty years, Mrs Chase. I make forty thousand dollars a year. And there's a big blackboard up here, and in the boss's own handwriting it says, "Any connection with or about Mary Chase. Highest priority. No exceptions." How's that, Mary Chase. It might just as well also say I've lost my job.'

'Don't be silly,' she commiserated. 'First of all, I don't blame you for being tired on Christmas Eve. Secondly, the little girl ran away from her grandmother in Newport. Third, she's safe with me. Fourth, I want very much to speak to Bruce—to Mr Latimore, and I don't know how to do it. And fifth, I don't even know your name, so how will he ever find out?'

'Whoa!' he returned. 'I thought—well, what we've heard about you, Mrs Chase, and the road, you know—well, hell. Give me your telephone number and I'll have him call you back. It'll take some time, you understand. That's a big country out there, and it's only about—well, it's six o'clock in the morning out there. He'll call you.'

'That's good of you, Mr——?'

'Riley,' he supplied the name automatically, and then seemed to be choking.

'Don't worry,' she told him. 'I've got a terrible memory for names. Merry Christmas, Mr—er—Smith.'

It was almost midnight before the tree decorations were complete. Mary chased the two younger girls off to bed, while Henry and Anna filled the stockings and piled the wrapped gifts under the tree. When it was finished, they all shared a hot buttered rum, and the pair of them, warmed by more than the rum, went off to bed.

From practical experience Mary knew that Becky would be up early, to see what 'Santa' had brought. Although she had disclaimed belief when she was six years old, she had always been willing to reinstate herself among the Santa-followers at each Christmas time. But, even being tired, upset, and expectant of an early call in the morning, Mary Kate could not drive herself to go upstairs. He would call. He would certainly call! So she squirmed into the chair by the telephone, opened up her knitting bag, and knitted herself to sleep.

The telephone bell woke her at two in the morning. She let it ring three times, and then snatched it up. A female operator with a delightful accent assured herself that Mrs Chase was indeed on the line, and then there was a pause.

His voice came down the miles of wire and satellite circuits with a hollow boom. There must be storms all over the world, she thought as she listened. He's mad too!

'All right,' he snarled, 'what the hell is wrong now?'

'Thank you,' she murmured back. 'I'm well, and I hope you are too?'

'Mary?' The snarl had gone, but not the temper. 'I'm terribly busy. We're in the midst of a major sandstorm out here, and I've lost four pieces of equipment.'

Which, of course, was just enough of a match to light off her flame again. 'I'm sorry you lost your toys,' she said coldly. And then, four notes higher. 'You've lost some of them over here, too. We're in the middle of the worst blizzard in seventy years.'

'Yes,' he sighed, 'I heard. Is that what you wanted to tell me?'

'No. Your daughter ran away in the middle of the storm.' And now have I gotten your attention, Mr Latimore, she thought. Try that out instead of one of those terrible cigars!

'Mattie? She ran away during the blizzard? What happened?' All the arrogance had gone out of his voice.

'She ran away from her grandmother during the blizzard, and came to me. She's here now. She had a nip of frostbite on her toes, but that's all better now. She says her grandmother doesn't like her, and she won't go back.'

'Won't go back? Well of course she'll go back. What are you doing to me, Mary Kate. Encouraging a child to disobedience? Of course she'll go back. At once!'

'At once. Yes, sir! All the roads are closed, and won't be ploughed out for a week or more. I'll put her on my sledge, shall I, and tow her to Newport? It's only eighty miles as the crow flies. But they're not flying, either.'

'Well, whoa now,' he said gently. 'I didn't know——'

'Of course you didn't know,' she shouted at him. 'You never know. You just think you can wave your magic wand and everything will change to suit your fancy, and the sun will shine and the snow will melt, and all of us who love you will just quietly sit here until you condescend to notice that we're alive, don't you—you—imperious bastard!'

'What was that you said?' he retorted.

'Bastard!' she roared at him. 'My mother told me never to say a word like that, because it isn't ladylike, but then she never knew any real bastards!'

'Not that,' he laughed. 'Sticks and stones, and all that. What you said *before* that!'

'I said——' and then it came to her just what she had said, and she was caught between laughter and tears. Happy because she had said it, and, from his tone, he had wanted to hear it. Sad, because it had taken so long for her to know her own mind. 'I don't remember what I said,' she lied. 'But you'd better get—you'd better—if you want Mattie to go back to Newport, you're going to have to take her there yourself. And pretty soon, too. She's all broken up about it. It's Christmas right now, and no little girl should be without her father at Christmas. Whatever in the world were you thinking of! You'd just better get your butt over here as fast as you can, you hear me Mr Latimore?'

'I hear you, Mrs Chase,' he laughed. 'That's the finest Christmas present I ever had!'

'I wish I knew what you were talking about,' she

sighed. 'And when you come, bring a shovel. The road isn't ploughed yet, and——'

'And I should come all that long way because only Mattie needs me?' he interrupted.

'What do you want from me?' she asked querulously. 'A pound of flesh? Well, all right, I need you too. Does that satisfy you?'

'We'll have to see, won't we?' he returned. 'I'm coming. Give my regards to the Colonel.' She could hear the click as he hung up.

Give my regards to the Colonel. What in heaven's name could he mean by that? But he *was* coming. If he could take off in a sandstorm and land in a blizzard! She went over to the window and drew back the curtain. The snow had stopped for good. Through breaks in the clouds she could see the inverted Dipper pouring water down on Polaris. It was omen enough. She went upstairs, laughing to herself. Of course he would come. He could do *anything*!

And of course he did, but it took him more than twenty-four hours. In the meantime the family had risen early, opened presents, breakfasted, and gone out into the sun for a snowball fight. Mindful that cows knew no holidays, Henry hitched the plough to the tractor and ploughed paths between the farmhouses and the barns, and then had gone on to plough the county road up as far as Main Street, so the milk collection trucks could move. Anna returned to her own home, eager to take up her separate existence, and Becky and Mattie played in the snow until they were exhausted.

They dined on left-overs that night. The baked ham smothered in pineapple slices had been the centrepiece of the two o'clock dinner, and looked as if it might last until the New Year. There were enough mashed potatoes left over to guarantee potato-pancakes for a week, and nobody seemed to want the green vegetables. The two girls, dead tired, showered and laughed their way to bed. Mattie treasured the four-foot high stuffed bear that Mary had bought for her, and took it to bed. By ten o'clock the house was quiet. There was no wind. The temperature hovered around twenty degrees, and the sky was full of stars.

Mary sat in the living room, anticipating. Her nerves were a lost cause. Every sudden noise startled her. The sound of cars on the road in front of the house brought her running to the window. But none of them turned in at Somerfield Farms. By midnight the waiting had become too much for her. She shook off her panic and started to clear up the house. By two o'clock even that had palled. She left the porch light on and trailed upstairs into the shower. There was plenty of hot water, and she revelled in it, soaping herself sensuously, turning and spinning in the circle of the spray until satiated. The rush of water had deafened her temporarily. When she stepped out, the quiet of the winter world surrounded her again. She towelled vigorously, and was blow-drying her hair when a noise disturbed her. It sounded like a door slamming.

Did I leave the front door open, she asked herself. Probably not, but her routine habits had come unstuck over the past three days, and she would have to check. She grabbed at the big bath towel and wound it around her waist, as usual. She was already at the foot of the stairs before she realised she was not alone. Coming out of the living room, with a drink in his hand, was Bruce Latimore.

'Well,' he said gruffly, 'I thought the place was deserted. Where's Mattie?'

Why doesn't he come and kiss me, she thought. He can't keep his eyes off me, but he's as distant as—Saudi Arabia! Will I ever see the time when he's not angry with me? 'She's upstairs asleep,' she said dolefully. 'In the room at the head of the stairs.'

He nodded, an unreadable expression on his face. He

stopped for a second on the same stair as she, and devoured her with his eyes. 'Later,' he muttered, and bounded up the stairs two at a time. She turned to watch him, puzzled. He tiptoed into the room, and was gone for a minute. When he came back out his expression had changed. He wore a big grin.

'She looks okay,' he said.

'She *is* okay.'

'Okay. Now let's talk about you.'

'About me? What about me?'

'Item number one, Mary Chase, I want to *talk* to you. Item number two, I can't hardly do that as long as you're standing there almost naked. You've got one minute. Either get out of my sight, or get into my bed. Which?'

For the first time in a confusing ten minutes she realised that she was standing in front of him wearing nothing but a towel draped casually around her waist. She squeaked in alarm, and her hands jumped to cover her breasts. And that grin of his grew wider.

'That's no use, Mrs Chase,' he said. 'There's too much there to be hidden by one of your hands. Now, one of mine, perhaps, might do?' He reached out one hand in the general direction of her breast.

'No!' she squealed. 'No!' She backed away from him until her bottom bumped into the banister. And then she ran, ran as if her life depended on it, until she was safe inside her bedroom. Thoroughly confused, head whirling, she paced up and down the length of her room until she had her breath under control. Then she fumbled through her clothes. Something loose. Something to cover her from head to foot. Something to hide behind. She found it in a long zippered housecoat that fitted like a tent. Under it, despite her normal habits, she fitted a bra, briefs, and a half-slip. 'A corset is what I need,' she told her vanity-mirror reflection. Her mother had always worn a corset.

Hugging her, when she was fully dressed, was like hugging a suit of chain mail. 'Which is exactly what I need,' she affirmed. But of course she had nothing like that available. Her hair was still slightly damp, so she left it loose. Her face was bare of make-up, and she meant to leave it that way.

She walked down the stairs with her head held high. Keep your image, she lectured herself as she went. Princess Mary. The Wicked Stepmother. Mary the Magnificent. Whatever. The Ice Queen. Now that's the one! She strolled through into the living room looking almost composed, but feeling as shaky as a fourteen-year old on her first date. He was standing in the middle of the room, still clutching a drink.

He held it up in a sort of toast. 'My second,' he said. 'I hope you don't mind. It was one hell of a trip.'

'I don't mind,' she told him. She started for the armchair, but as she passed him his empty hand grabbed at her wrist, and he drew her to the couch and settled beside her. 'Tell me about it,' he commanded.

'Well,' she started out, 'It was late at night, and the blizzard was blowing, and I got this telephone call from Mattie, and——'

'Not that, damn it,' he interrupted grouchily. 'I can see she's okay. Tell me the important part.'

'Important part? I don't understand.'

'Of course you don't,' he laughed. 'You look to be about sixteen with your hair down. Is Becky really older than you?'

'Of course not,' she snapped. 'What a ridiculous thing to say. What are you doing?' The last part of the sentence came out as a squeak. What he was doing was to put both arms around her, to draw her down into his lap. Which, after the initial surprise, didn't seem such a bad idea at all! She tipped her head back to watch his unreadable face. With a contented sigh she leaned against his chest, with his heart just under her ear.

'I'm waiting,' he prodded her.

'Waiting for what?'

'I'm waiting for you to tell me why you missed me.'

'Oh that.'

'Yes, that!'

'I—well—I was thinking things over.'

'And?'

'And I thought—Mattie said—it would be easiest for all of us if I—if we were to get married.'

'Smart girl that. Her father's only daughter. So far.'

'So far?' She was squeaking again, and couldn't stop it.

'And what do you think?'

'Well, I thought it over very carefully. It would be good for Mattie to have a mother. And I suppose you could use a wife—because of all your work, you know—but then I had to think of Becky. She's too young to be left, and too old to be moved from pillar to post, and I have to talk to her, and——'

He concluded her argument by kissing her gently but thoroughly. When he released her, she was breathless. 'That's all very logical,' he said softly. 'But how about you—and the Colonel?'

She struggled to move away from him, her spine straight, head bowed to shield her face from his spying eyes. 'The Colonel was a fine man,' she said softly, 'but he's dead.'

He tipped her face up, with one finger under her chin. 'You're sure?' he asked.

'Yes, I'm very sure,' she replied. 'You were right in a way. I had picked up his mantle, and invested my life in his goals. Becky and Henry. I still love them dearly, but the Colonel is dead.'

'I accept that,' he returned, 'and so that leaves only you!'

'Yes,' she sighed. 'I love you.'

'And that is the end of the tale of the Wicked

Stepmother,' he chortled. He pulled her back against him, running a hand through her hair, twisting little tendrils into curls, and then he turned her and kissed her again. There were no flames, she told herself. The books all lie. Just comfort, pleasure, peace. She snuggled down against him, content that it should be so. And then, it seemed almost by accident, his fingers trailed up from the curve of her hip and touched the peak of her breast. And the world went up in flames! She heard herself moan as she scrabbled against him, prying at the buttons of his shirt, both hands clawing for access. She hardly noticed when his hand slashed at the long zipper of her housecoat, and that garment fell off her shoulders and piled itself at her waist. Her own hands were inside his shirt, running up and down, from beltline to neck, and she was shaking, shaking.

But when her bra disappeared, snatched off by his impatient hand, and he leaned over to seize her nipple with a roving tongue, she gave up her own pursuits and surrendered to the rending pleasures that assailed her. Somewhere in the distance she could hear some fool muttering 'Bruce!' over and over again. She moaned as his hand, following the line of least resistance, slipped down over the outline of her slightly rounded stomach, and on to her hips. She was barely on the edge of reality when some other fool knocked over the floor lamp, but its resounding crash attracted only a portion of her fragmented mind. She was lying half on his lap, half on the couch, when his hand reached for the band of her briefs. She sucked in her stomach in piercing anticipation, when a voice penetrated the mists.

'Daddy! Daddy, you're here!' Mattie was at the door. He stood up abruptly, whirling Mary Kate around behind him, hiding her with his bulk. She pressed up against his back, dazed and trying to catch her breath, and watched as the little girl hurled herself across the room and into his arms. And then reality hit! Mary blushed from head to toe, snatched at her errant housecoat, and managed to slide into it.

'What are you doing there, Ma?' the little girl enquired. Mary shook her head, unable to muster words through her dry throat.

'She's looking for my pen,' he lied. 'I dropped it.'

'Oh that's silly, Ma. Come up here with me and we'll both kiss him. That'll teach him a lesson.'

'It certainly will,' she managed to murmur as she pecked at his cheek.

'Ma? You look like you're all out of breath,' Mattie said.

'She is. She is. But you've got to go back to bed,' her father told her. To the surprise of them both the little girl smiled and ran back up the stairs. They stood at the foot, hand in hand, watching until the bedroom door closed behind her.

'Mrs Chase?' he murmured into her hair.

'Hmmm?'

'Who'd ever think that the kitten would turn into a tigress. I think we'd better get married.'

She moved closer, against the iron wall of him, the protective, solid, loving wall. 'I will if you will,' she said softly. 'But very quickly, please, Mr Latimore. Very quickly!'

CHAPTER SEVEN

BUT saying 'quickly' was one thing, and doing it was another. The first problem, of course, was Becky. Mary went about it very diplomatically. The school holiday lasted until the third day of the new year, and Mattie and her father had gone off on a one-day trip to placate grandmother. At nine o'clock Mary made up two cups of coffee and took them up to Becky's room.

The place looked like a disaster area, with both girls' clothing hanging over chairs, lying in piles on the floor, or decorating the bureau in clumps. Becky was not to be seen. There was a hump in the middle of her bed, and her head was under the pillow.

'Awful,' Mary sighed.

The pillow shifted four inches, and an eye appeared. 'Ma? Oh, you mean the room?'

'It looks just like when I used to sleep here,' Mary told her. 'Only I had the extra bed to pile things on. You want some coffee?'

'Coffee? In bed? Am I sick?' Becky wiggled herself carefully out of the cocoon of blankets and sat up. And look what's happened to style, Mary told herself. The girl had given up lace and nightgowns and pyjamas, and was sleeping in a man's T-shirt marked 'Property of the Boston Celtics'. But no basketball player had ever fitted into this one. It clung to the girl's developing figure like a second skin, and the price paid for it would have bought four full-length flannel nightgowns. Which is something I won't need very much longer, she thought. I wonder if he sleeps in pyjamas? Or anything? Well, I'll keep one flannel nightgown, anyway. Some night there might be a fire.

'Ma? The coffee?'

'Oh my,' she laughed. 'I was day-dreaming. Here you are, pet.' Becky took the cup and settled herself back against the carved wooden headboard, a memento of the Colonel's three-year tour in Germany.

'And you were saying, Ma?'

'I guess I really wasn't, was I,' she laughed. 'I don't know what's come over me.'

'Don't you, Ma? I do. Why don't you stop mooning around and marry the guy?'

'Well—I—you really think I should?'

'I really think you'd better, Ma. And pretty quickly, too.'

'What *are* you talking about,' Mary stuttered.

'Come off it, Ma. The other night when the lamp was knocked over I came downstairs right behind Mattie. But I had the common sense to duck back upstairs. Boy, he was already at third base and heading for home plate, wasn't he!'

'Well really!' Mary muttered. And then, when her face had returned to a more normal colour. 'You do think marriage would be a good idea?'

'Best idea going this year. And Henry thinks so too.'

'Henry? You told Henry?'

'Why of course. Who else would have a major interest besides me and Henry? And Mattie, of course. It's a great idea. When?'

'We—there isn't a date set yet,' she burbled. 'There's a problem, Becky. I agreed to marry him, but there's a condition. What about you, sweetheart?'

'Me? What about me? You've been my mother since I was five years old. You don't plan to give me up, do you?'

'Of course I don't, dear. But you're old enough to make choices. And I think you deserve them. First of all, if you're absolutely against it, I shan't marry him at all!'

'That's silly. It's better to marry than to burn. Isn't that what the Bible says. What other choices do I have?'

'If you agree to the wedding, you can go to Henry and Anna, or you can stay here in your own house with a housekeeper, or you can come and live with Bruce and Mattie and myself.'

'Hey, that's no choice,' Becky said. 'You're where all the action is, Ma. I want to go with you—if he doesn't object?'

'He won't have a chance to object,' Mary responded. 'I'll tell him it's a package deal. Two for the price of one. Love me, love my Becky.' Which earned her an immediate hug that spilled coffee all over the grey carpet on the floor, and left them both laughing.

That night, while she was recounting the story to Bruce, she kept an eye on his face, looking for some sign, some signal. She was rewarded by a wide-spread grin. 'Why of course,' he said. 'With Becky in the house we'll have a live-in babysitter! So now, when do we get married?'

She thought she had the answer when she met the family on New Year's Day. The party the night before had been limited. The snow still held the roads in its icy grip, and more was threatening. They were all in fine spirits. Mattie and Becky shared the couch. Henry was in the love seat with Anna. Bruce was in the heavy armchair. They all looked at her expectantly.

'I thought we should keep it simple,' she started out. They all smiled and nodded. 'I thought we would go into Taunton and be married by the Clerk of the District Court. Then we could have a small——' There was too much noise for her to continue.

'No, no, no,' Becky was chanting. Mattie had lost track of the discussion, but joined in the chant anyway.

'No indeed,' Anna said very firmly. The girls stopped to hear what she had to say.

'First of all,' she said, 'you can't make it appear as if

you've something to hide. We are all church-goers, and I've always wanted to be a bridesmaid—or matron of honour—or whatever you call it, and there aren't many more opportunities.'

'Me too,' Becky yelled. 'I want to be a bridesmaid at my mother's wedding!'

'Don't be a wise guy,' Henry said, looking his sister to silence with a stare. 'I kind of like the church too. I could give you away, Ma. How about that! Church wedding!'

'Take a vote,' Becky yelled, the bit firmly between her teeth. 'Vote! Vote! This is a democracy. Everybody in favour of a church wedding raise their hand!' Five hands went up immediately.

Mary looked over to Bruce, hoping for some guidance, some help. He sat there with a smile on his face, and his voting hand up in the air. Abandoned by everyone, she was still not prepared to give in.

'After all, it's *my* wedding,' she said sadly. 'Don't I have anything to say?'

'Of course you do, darling,' Bruce said. 'Cast your vote.'

When she raised her head to look at him there was a smile playing around the corners of his mouth. She looked around the room at all these people who loved her, then slowly raised her own hand. And thereby tripled her problems!

'January is just the wrong month for weddings,' the pastor told her. 'There's always a weather problem, and transportation difficulties, and parking, and vacations. You know the organist will be away for two weeks at the beginning of the month, and I have my vacation planned for the last two weeks, and we have Epiphany, and there will be flu in the village for sure. Do you know what would make a perfect day for your wedding, Mary?'

She looked at him in astonishment. She had known

him all her life, having been baptized in his arms, and confirmed in the church at fourteen. During all that time he had been the same lean slightly-stooped, absent-minded man, whose wife trailed him from pillar to post, making sure he was properly dressed, and in the right place at the right time. And now—'Do you know what would make a perfect day for your wedding, Mary?'

'No, I guess I don't,' she admitted.

'St Valentine's Day,' he laughed. 'February 14th. The day for lovers. How about that?'

'But it's so—so long until then,' she started to protest. He leaned forward over his desk and lifted his glasses to his forehead. 'Are you telling me, Mary Katherine, that you *have* to get married sooner than February 14th?'

'Oh no! Not—no!' she repeated.

'Then in that case I'll write it in my book,' he said, and did so. His fingers were not as flexible as they once had been. Arthritis bent two of them unmercifully, but he gritted his teeth and printed in the calendar, repeating aloud, 'Marriage Mary Katherine Chase, and Bruce P. Latimore. There. What does the P. stand for, Mary?'

'I don't know,' she admitted. And when she told him the whole story that night she still didn't find out. He evaded her question with some of his own. And then she had to run, for it was one of her school nights. He was more possessive than he had been before. 'Why don't you just junk that school,' he asked as he helped her on with her coat. 'You know all you need to know to be Mrs Bruce Latimore.'

'That may be,' she teased him, 'But I don't know all I need to know to be Mrs Mary Latimore. What does the P. stand for?'

'What the devil are you studying?' he countered.

She had no intention of telling him. Somehow or another it seemed important that he did not find out who the real culprit was behind all those delays in his roadbuilding. So neither question was answered. At least not that night.

If you plan a church wedding, you have to invite people. Mary almost cried the night the family finally agreed on who would be invited. Not that she was really for or against anyone on the list, except for Mr Collyer. When Mary was fifteen he had caught her raiding his grapevine, and had blistered her bottom for her, so much so that she couldn't sit down for three days. What really bothered her was that each night they met, some new name *had* to be added to the list. So when they closed the proceedings the numbers stood at two hundred and sixteen people. And so much for her *little* wedding! She was beginning to feel like one of the Christians, penned in a cell under the Roman Arena, waiting to join the lions for lunch. She went to bed that night and cried herself to sleep.

And after the invitations went out, came the oddities. Check with the sexton—and the town police—about parking. And how do we clear snow from the parking lot? We tell Bruce, and he gives orders for two Latimore Corporation snow ploughs to be in the village, starting three days before the wedding!

The matter of dresses, which Mary really feared, was mentioned to Bruce on Friday night. On the next Wednesday morning an elderly woman accompanied by three younger girls appeared at the door. Operating in a half-speed daze, Mary opened the door warily.

'Dresses,' the elderly woman said quietly. Mary looked back at her with a blank expression on her face. 'Dresses,' the woman repeated. 'From the Latimore Corporation, no? Dresses?'

'You—you sell dresses?' Mary stammered.

The lady gave her a haughty smile. 'We *make* dresses,' she said, as if the word 'sell' left a bad taste in her mouth. 'Mr Latimore sends me, no?' At the word

Latimore she allowed a tiny smile to appear on her frosty face.

'Mr Latimore, yes,' Mary sighed, and ushered them into the living room. As she followed the quartet her mind began to spin. By the time we get married, she thought, I'll be a shadow, a dark shadow, tiptoeing around his house, standing quietly in corners when he wants to shut me off. And all the biddies down at the post office will be saying 'I wonder what ever became of Mary Chase?' And I'll have to practise saying 'Yes sir' and 'right away sir' and things like that. Why would he want to marry *me*?

But it was really true that Mrs Frangini made dresses. She sat with all the women, searching for agreement as to styles, then watched as her assistants took measurements, and promised to return in one week. Which she did.

The bridal gown took Mary's breath away the moment she saw it. Cut from cream velvet—one needs to be warm in a church in February, Mrs Frangini had assured her—it was cut in the princess line, with a full length skirt, and a heart-shaped neckline, trimmed with crystal beads. The sleeves were long and fitted over the wrists, with little twists of lace around the edges. The whole was topped by a featherweight veil, suspended from an almost invisible gold coronet. Anna and Becky's dresses followed the same design, but were made up from cranberry velvet, with white lace edgings on the neck and sleeves. Mattie, who was to serve as flower-girl, was outfitted in a full-length cranberry velvet, with a pattern of lace running around the skirt some two inches above the hem, and a white lace Bertha collar.

All of which she found very difficult to explain to Bruce on that first day of February when the dresses received their final fitting. He hardly seemed interested. At least in the dresses, that is. Every time she tried to get his attention he would lean down and kiss her. And it was strange. His kisses were no longer placid, sweet, restful. Every time he touched her—anywhere—it was 'Katie bar the door!' Even a casual chuck under the chin by one of his big fingers would turn her on, shooting her out into orbit. And he knew it, damn the man!

'You sure you can wait out the week?' he whispered in her ear.

'No, I'm not sure, darn you,' she snarled back at him. 'Down boy! Back to your cage!'

'Be brave,' he laughed. 'Be independent. Come tomorrow-week you'll get yours, let me tell you.'

'We'll see,' she returned smartly. 'We'll see who does what to whom!'

'Whom?' he laughed. 'How prissy can you get. You're not afraid of me, are you?'

'Of course not,' she retorted. But she took very great care to move a safe distance away from him, and to be sure that someone else was in the house when he came calling during that last week. Because deep down, where it really mattered, she knew very well that she was a little—just a little bit—afraid of him.

And so they were married.

For a week she worried about the weather. Movements, cars, crowds, all depended on the weather. And luck. From Anna's mother she heard the one about rain making a bride happy. From Mrs Bethel, the wife of the pastor, she heard *happy is the bride the sun shines on.* But when she came carefully down the stairs on that fateful Wednesday, it was snowing again. When she groaned, Henry laughed.

'Don't worry, Ma,' he said, 'We'll get you to the church on time.' She sighed and shook her head at him. Dear, dear man. What the devil did *he* know about *lucky is the bride*?

But at the proper time the entire party loaded up in the four limousines that Bruce had imported from

Boston, and they went merrily on their way, preceded by a snow plough. She craned her neck when they reached the church, and sure enough, the snow plough, which had pulled off into a corner of the cleared parking lot, was marked Latimore Corporation. Henry, catching her eye, said, 'Well, he's a very thorough man. Never leaves anything to chance, that one.'

She was in a fine state of nerves as her little cortège formed up in the outer lobby of the church. What am I doing, she asked herself. I'm going to marry the Latimore Corporation, Inc. I'm going to end up as Mrs Latimore Inc. And he'll put a sign on me somewhere that says 'Property of Latimore Coporation', and then—oh dear God help me—why is he marrying me? Just then Henry took her arm. Dear dependable Henry. The doors were thrown open and she stood there, with Mattie and Becky and Anna in front of her. She stood there, and could not, for the life of her, move her knees.

'Last chance,' Henry whispered in her ear. 'If you want to run, now's the time!' Which gave her a case of the giggles, released all her stuck joints, and the organ music swelled as they walked down the aisle.

There were a crowd of people at the altar, or so it seemed through the interstices of her veil. That's what the veil is for, she told herself. Not to hide my face, but to keep me from seeing what I'm getting into! What a wise custom! But by that time they had reached the chancery rail and stopped. Henry leaned down and lifted her veil, kissed her on her cheek, and placed her hand in Bruce's.

And then people came and went, and said things to which she must have made the right response, but for the life of her she could not remember what was going on. Love, honour, and cherish. With this ring I do thee wed. Through it all she had eyes only for him. She burned his expression into her brain, smiled when he glanced at her, felt an all-enveloping glow as he slipped the gold ring on her finger, and surrendered shamelessly when he kissed her. And it was over.

They walked back up the aisle arm in arm to more heavy music from the organ. She felt like skipping. He pulled her down to a more pedestrian walk. 'Take it easy,' he whispered in her ear. 'We still have to get out the door without God striking me dead!'

'Why would he want to do that?' she whispered back.

'Because I've stolen one of his angels, and he doesn't know it yet!' he returned. She pinched his arm hard. After all, it was blasphemy—although of the very most pleasant kind—but then perhaps that was the trouble with the world—its sins and blasphemies were *too* pleasant!

When they reached the door he introduced her to his best man, a somewhat shorter and stouter version of himself. 'My best man,' he said. 'And my right hand in the business, Charlie Riley.' Riley wasted no time. He came around the party, latched on to the bride, and exacted his payment with enthusiasm. As he started to pull away she put one hand around his neck and whispered in his ear, 'Made any nice telephone calls lately, Mr Riley?'

He shook his head and laughed as he pulled away. She laughed back at him, but when she turned her head she saw her new husband glaring at her, and she almost swallowed her tongue. No doubt about it, Mary—er—Latimore, she told herself, there's a new master on the plantation from now on, and you'd better shape up, kid!

They used the limousines to travel the two blocks of Main Street to the Veterans of Foreign Wars Hall. A Latimore snow plough had cleared the entire way, of course. They spent an hour among what seemed to be five thousand people, although that couldn't be. The hall only held five hundred. The cake was cut, toasts were drunk, and she slipped away upstairs to where a private room had been set aside for her. With her three girls around her, she catechised them as they helped her change. 'And Becky, you be sure to watch out for Mattie, and you both do exactly what Anna tells you, and don't give her a minute of trouble—and—and I do wish you all could come with us!'

Which of course brought on tears. Everyone cried, wished her well, and rushed her downstairs into the hands of her very impatient husband.

He was standing at the door of a new Mercedes, tapping his fingers on the windshield, looking like Jupiter enraged. She was apologising before she even reached him. 'I'm sorry, dear,' she said. 'We were getting ready, and everything, and then we just all had to have a good cry. Please don't be angry?'

'I'm not angry with you,' he said solemnly. 'It's this damn weather. Now they're forecasting eight inches of snow. Did you know, despite the fact we've been studying the problem for six years, Latimore Corporation has not yet been able to control the weather!' It all sounded so damnably pompous that she looked up in surprise, only to see a broad grin stretching from ear to ear across his dear face.

'Well!' was all she could think of to say. He opened the door of the car and pushed her into the warm interior. Party goers yelled raucous suggestions, horns blew, somebody threw a paper bag full of rice, and then they were off.

So, what *do* you say to a brand new husband driving a heavy car westward through a miniature blizzard? Drive faster, I hear they have a beautiful view at this health resort in the Berkshires? Did you remember to put out the cat? Stop right here, there's plenty of room in the back seat? Or a simple compromise.

'My, wasn't that a nice service?'

'Yes. Very.'

A few more wind-battered miles passed under the

wheels of the shiny car. There's a thought. 'New car?' she asked.

'Yes,' he replied. And a dozen more miles passed under the wheels.

'Well, don't you want to talk at all?' she pouted at him.

'Yes. I want to talk. What I want to say is let's pull over. There's plenty of room in the back seat! But this damn storm is driving me up the wall. I rate it just below you—for driving me up the wall, I mean. Look here, we're never going to make the Berkshires in this stuff. We're at Stockbridge now, and there's a good motel up there ahead of us. How about it?'

'I don't mind if you don't mind,' she said nervously.

'I mind,' he said. He pulled in under the marquee of the motel, engaged a room, and they followed the bellhop down the corridor to a corner room on the first floor. She trailed behind them through the door, and into a large, square room, full of brightness. The entire corner wall was a sliding floor-to-ceiling window, with a snow covered balcony outside. Even at the height of the storm light poured in and sparkled off the blue carpet, the yellow lemon walls, and darker glow of polished furniture. She watched cautiously as Bruce dealt with the bellboy and closed the door behind him. There was an itch piling up under her scalp. Something had changed suddenly. Yesterday he had been her friend, her confidant, her lover. Today he was her husband, invested with rights and privileges. Until death do us part!

She backed away from him, around the huge king-size bed, as he picked up one of the advertising leaflets from the bureau. 'Indoor heated swimming pool,' he chuckled, thumping the paper down. 'What's the matter, love?'

'I—I don't really know,' she replied huskily. 'It's not as if I were some kidnapped virgin. I—yesterday I could

talk to you easily—today I've got cotton in my mouth.
I have the feeling that while we were in church
somebody built a wall up between us.'

'I understand,' he said softly. 'There's the wall, right
there.' He gestured casually towards the bed. 'We have to
tear it down, Mary. That's what honeymoons are for.
Least said, soonest mended. You've heard that old saying?'

'I-it sounds so—mechanical,' she sighed.

'But? There is a but isn't there?'

'But? Yes, my dear. I'm an old-fashioned woman. I
probably should have said love, honour and obey.
That's my style. I shall do whatever you want me to.'

He checked the gold watch on his wrist. 'Four
o'clock,' he announced. 'Dinner is served from six to
eight. Why don't you have a shower, then lie down. I'm
going back to the desk for some cigars and a bottle of
bubbly.'

He was gone before she could muster a protest. She
snapped open her smaller bag, pulled out bath
equipment, and went into the attached bathroom for a
shower. When he came back she was half asleep, under
a sheet, with the rest of the blankets thrown down at
the foot of the bed.

'Be with you in a minute,' he said as he dashed into
the bathroom. He was out in less than five minutes, hair
still gleaming wet, covered only by a towel around his
waist. She watched him under half-closed eyelashes. A
sign of the impatient male? she asked herself. It's been
so long. Will it hurt as badly as it did the first time?

'Hey,' he laughed as he slid into the bed beside her.
'You're lying at attention. Relax.'

'Easy for you to say,' she grumbled, and then gasped.
With one swoop of his arm her covering sheet was
discarded, and they were both stretched out, nude. She
could hear him suck in his breath sharply. His eyes
ravaged her, and she could see the hunter's look in his
eye. A tingle of raw fear ran up her spine.

'What's the matter?' he asked softly. His mouth was at her ear, and one hand was toying with her hair.

'It's—just—well, I've never—not in the daylight,' she muttered. 'It was always—in the dark. Could we close the curtains?'

'Not on your life,' he chuckled. 'I want to worship you. Like this!' He slid himself down to the foot of her bed and picked up one of her small feet in his hand. As he kissed each of her toes she felt another shiver, and then a giggle as his spare hand tickled the bottom of her other foot. 'That's better,' he said. 'You're relaxing. Those are beautiful feet.'

'Of course,' she returned, trying to get into the spirit. 'Unique.'

'Unique?'

'Surely. Of all the billions of people in the world today I am the only one allowed to walk on those feet.'

'Oh?' he queried. 'Female logic? Look at those knees. Magnificent!' He kissed one gently, then the other, running his fingers up and down from her ankle to her knee. 'Very proud knees,' he murmured. 'They only bend one way?'

'Yes,' she chuckled, 'and only for you, my lord.'

'And master,' he added. 'Very commendable. You'll make a good wife if only I remember to beat you occasionally. Why are you jumping like that?'

'Your hand,' she sputtered, looking at the offending extension slowly creeping up the inside of her thigh. 'Don't do that unless you mean it!'

'Oh I mean it, little lady,' he threatened. But the hand kept climbing. It glided up her thigh, across her groin and up to where her ample hips curved sharply inward to her waist. 'And now, dear friends,' he intoned, mocking the voice of the pastor. 'A tiny waist, and marvellously constructed hips. Look at that. Just built for a man's comfort!'

'You missed a great deal of territory,' she gasped at

him. It was becoming exceedingly hard for her to breathe.

'I intended to come back,' he assured her. And then the wandering hand moved upward, climbing the slope of her breast, and stopping, triumphant at her proud throbbing nipple. At which time the world exploded, her calm demeanour splintered into ten million pieces and she lay there like a demented Lorelei, happily assisting in her own demolition!

She woke up some time later, feeling as self-satisfied as any Tabby at the fireplace. He tapped her on the shoulder. 'It's half past dinner time,' he told her.

She tried to open both eyes at the same time, to savour all of him. 'Oh my goodness, Bruce,' she cried, and sat up so violently it almost knocked him off the bed. 'Those scratches! Who did that to you?'

'Hey, don't be so aggressive,' he chuckled. 'It served me right, and she's been adequately punished.'

'She?' Her face turned rose-red. 'You mean I——' And for the first time she felt how tender her breasts were, and how much her hips ached. 'Yes,' he laughed back at her, 'She's been punished enough—for now, that is! Did you enjoy your evening—so far?'

She cocked an eye up at him. 'What do you think?' she returned.

'Well, I don't know,' he said quietly. 'I'm always afraid of comparisons. The Colonel?'

She sat up and looked him straight in the eye. 'Who?' she asked.

He had the grace to blush. She reached over for one of his hands. 'You must never do that,' she told him softly. 'You had a wife; I had a husband. We must never compare. They were—different, and they're both gone. And now we are us—together. Never compare. Never.'

'Yes,' he agreed. 'How lucky can I get. A beautiful, sweet, understanding, intelligent wife!'

'You said it,' she agreed laughingly, 'and don't forget that when times get tough!'

And so they learned to play together, to love together, to grow together. They showered together and laughed when the chambermaid complained about wet sheets. They swam together in the heated pool, playing children's games. They spent hours across a coffee table from each other, mooning like a pair of adolescents. They ate fine, expensive food, and hardly tasted a thing except each other. And four days after the storm had swept out into the Atlantic Ocean they were still at the motel in Stockbridge, and it was their last day, Sunday.

'I've got to go home,' he groaned as she lay on the bed, laughing at him. 'I've got to get back to work, so I can have a rest!'

'Come here, Tiger,' she chuckled, 'Mama wants to have another word with you.'

'Not again,' he moaned. 'Is there no satisfying you, woman?'

'Me?' she asked innocently. 'What happened to all those threats—about what you were going to do? What happened to Superman?'

He flopped down on the bed beside her, fully clothed. 'All right, Wonder Woman,' he said. 'I give up. I'll go quietly.'

She toyed with a lock of his usually immaculate hair, twisting it around her finger. 'You know,' she said casually, 'I was talking to the desk clerk this morning?'

'Oh? What about?' He spoke cautiously, as if he really didn't want to hear.

'He was telling me how lucky we were that we had phoned ahead last week for reservations. For the entire week, he said.'

'Oh. Yes, that was fortunate,' he said weakly.

'Wasn't it, you big fraud!' She rolled over on top of him, pinioned his face with both her hands, and kissed him thoroughly. 'You never intended to get to the Berkshires, did you!'

'It was all that scenery and do-gooding,' he complained. 'You'd get up there in the mountains, and you'd want to go see the sights, and take long walks in the snow, and maybe ski, and all that.'

'I certainly would have,' she said in an injured tone of voice. 'What's wrong with that?'

'It's my honeymoon. I hadn't intended to let you set foot on the floor, or ever get out of bed at all! And I certainly didn't want to have to compete with views of mountains!'

'Aha!' she chortled. 'A consummate faker, Bruce Latimore. So you laid on this elaborate trap, and then found you couldn't stay the course, could you.'

'What the devil do you mean,' he roared in injured innocence. 'I can stay the course, lady. Right now, you hear me?'

'I hear you,' she retorted, trying to sound fearful. But when he pushed her down into the soft mattress there was a half-concealed smile on her anticipating lips.

All of which delayed their departure from Stockbridge until four o'clock in the afternoon. The weather had changed. The snow was almost evaporating before their eyes, and all the tiny rivers of central Massachusetts were overflowing their banks.

'January thaw,' he commented, as they moved into the high-speed traffic lane.

'Of course,' she agreed humbly. 'It's February 21st.'

He brushed it off as unimportant. The sun followed them all the way home, but it was a weak and watery winter sun, and it had nothing to sparkle on. The maple and oak trees along the road stuck their empty branches up like spear-carriers in a long-dead legion, and the only birds in sight were pigeons and English sparrows.

They went through the centre of Eastboro at about seven o'clock. Not a light was to be seen on Main

Street, and only occasionally a twinkle could be seen in the distance, behind winter curtains and wooden shutters. Not a soul was out on the streets. A cold, bleak, New England winter night.

They pulled off the road and up the circular drive that led to the old house—which to her was the new house—home? As soon as the engine was heard, the front door of the house swung open, casting a fan of light across the darkness. Mary Kate barely had the car door open when Mattie, without coat or sweater, scrambled down the stairs and threw herself in her outstretched arms. Mary hugged her close, watching over Mattie's curl-topped head to where Becky was following more sedately. As Mattie burrowed into her shoulder, Becky leaned over and kissed her mother's nose, an old and secret custom between them that sealed their bond of love. Mattie was crying excitedly. Mary Kate soothed her gently, maintaining the pressure of her arms around the little girl, but all the while studying Becky as the tall, thin almost-woman turned towards Bruce, who had walked around the front of the car and now stood by the door.

It was a testing time. Mary held her breath, nibbled at her lower lip, with her eyes glued to Becky's excited face. The girl looked up at the tall shadow of the man who now held all their lives in thrall. Becky stood straight and tall, shoulders thrown back, hands clasped behind her. 'Hi Pop,' she said softly.

The man stooped towards her, swept her up in his arms, and whirled her around in a complete circle. Her cheek was pressed hard against his, and as they turned Mary could see tears in Becky's eyes. 'Hi daughter,' he said, and the girl's face lit up with the light of a thousand stars.

'Thank you Lord Jesus,' Mary whispered into the curls of the still snuggling Mattie. 'It's going to be all right!'

CHAPTER EIGHT

SHE found it hard to settle down. For five years she had been her own woman, settling all issues, at the beck and call of no one. And now, suddenly, she was mistress of a tremendous old house, with a cook and a daily cleaner, and two growing daughters, each of whom must receive equal portions of love, advice and direction. And there was a man in residence.

He left the routine of the house to her, turning over the keys of authority with a sigh of relief. But whatever she did, she never was able to shake off the idea that he was a phantom looking over her shoulder, the dragon capable of destroying all her plans whenever he came out of his cave. Surprisingly, it was only at night that she felt sure of herself. Only when they went up to the master bedroom, closed the door and shut all the world's problems outside. Downstairs he might grumble when she disturbed his routine. Upstairs he was still the tender lover.

She rambled around the house for three days. It was one of the landmarks of Eastboro, having been built in 1795. Some Victorian ancestor of the original family had added a great gingerbread tower to the north side, but on the whole, its frame clapboard three storeys were much as originally planned—from the outside. Inside, a great deal of money and sacrifice had turned the old colonial cupboards into three bathrooms, on one each floor, and an additional one included in the master suite. Dormers outlined unused attic space, jammed with all the remembrances of families that had lived in the house. And then he had had the kitchen remodelled, so that it gleamed with futuristic panels and lights.

Her first little shock came from Mattie. The little girl came home at the weekend with an invitation for Mary to attend a school play on the next Monday.

'I just come?' she asked. Becky, who had been a very independent little miss, had never wanted to have her at school functions.

'You just come,' Mattie said. 'Did you know I was the only girl in my class with no mother, and now I got one, so you gotta come, huh?'

'Huh is right, Ma,' Becky laughed. 'Boy have you been getting away with murder!'

So on Monday she got out her old Mustang, and banged and rattled her way over to the Mary Queen of Heaven Parochial School, and was welcomed like a queen. And then had to squeeze into a child-size chair to watch a pageant of twelve episodes, during which Mattie appeared twice.

'We never seem to have enough boys to go around,' the nun confided in her, while coffee and cake were being served. Mary stayed late as part of the clean-up crew, giving a hand from time to time, answering questions like 'Was Mattie *really* the flower girl at your wedding? When my mother got married I wasn't even born yet!'

'And thank God for that,' Mary whispered under her breath as she fought off the inquisition. By four o'clock the work was finished, and she and Mattie were clanking down the road towards home. But they clanked only as far as Bushrod Crossing, about three miles from home, and there the Mustang gave up the ghost.

'Oh damn!' she muttered under her breath. Her practical brain reviewed the options. There was a roadside telephone booth just in sight at the crossroads. She could call Bill Miliken, and have him come and tow the car away. Or she could call Henry—but the cows would all be in the barn for milking at this hour. Or she could walk the three miles to Eastboro, or—she giggled as the newest idea struck her. What the heck, it's almost quarter to five!

'Mattie,' she said, fishing through her purse. 'Here's a dime. Be a good girl and go over to that telephone and call your father.'

'Sure. What'll I tell him, Ma?'

'Just tell him that we're stuck at the crossroads, baby. That's what fathers are for!'

He arrived in about twenty minutes, looked down his nose rather disdainfully at the Mustang, bundled them both into his Mercedes, and away they went. *See*, she told herself!

'But what are we gonna do about your car, Ma,' Mattie asked.

'We?' Mary laughed. I don't know. That's up to Daddy.'

There was a crinkly smile around the corners of his eyes as he reached over and patted her knee. 'Don't overdo it, lady,' he said, 'I'm not *your* daddy. And as for the Mustang, we're going to junk it. I had forgotten about that prehistoric relic.'

'But I've got to have a car to go to school with,' she hurriedly protested. Her little joke was about to blow up in her face!

'Not to worry,' he chuckled. 'That's what husbands are for—the worrying. You've got the right sheet of music, wife Mary, but you're just not accustomed to singing these notes, are you!' And I'm not, she told herself fiercely. I'm just as independent as I've ever been, but isn't it nice to have *him* do the worrying?

He was as good as his word, but a little slow—for him. Nothing happened on Tuesday, and that night he drove her to Boston himself, and waited for her after class. It took a little doing. She still had no intention of letting him know that she was studying at the New England School of Law. In the end she convinced him to drop her off at the Prudential building, and she took a cab from there. But on Wednesday morning, while she was still busily trying to decide whether to watch Jennie make beds, or Mrs Pemm start dinner, two young men from the local Ford agency drove up with a new four-door station wagon, and apologised for not having it available the day before.

'We have them in stock,' one of the men explained, 'but your husband was fussy about the safety features, and we had to make a deal with another dealer. This one has the experimental airbags in it.'

When he came home that night they sat together in the lounge, in front of a brisk oak-log fire, while the girls attacked their homework in the study. The companionship was improving Becky's grades. She told him all about it, sitting on a pillow at his feet, her arms resting on his knee. This was the position in which they both felt comfortable, and it had become a part of the family routine. He leaned back in his big chair and smiled comfortably at her, ruffling his fingers through her loose hair. 'But you shouldn't have bought such a big car,' she added. 'I'm used to something smaller. I might have an accident.'

'You might,' he commented. 'And then again you might not. All I know is that when some little compact cars have an accident, they get smashed all to pieces. If you're going to have an accident, I want you surrounded by all that steel plate. You're important to me, lady.'

'And you to me,' she sighed gently as she lay her head on his lap.

Late the next morning began the chain of circumstances that finally tipped over her barrow, and spilled all her happiness down the drain. Charlie Momson telephoned.

'Mary Kate,' he said when she finally struggled down to the telephone. 'I've got some news, and I don't know if it's good or bad.'

'Okay Charlie,' she chuckled, 'lay it on me, and we'll see, won't we.'

'All right, I will. Incidentally, I've been calling for two days, and following the old adage, if a man answers, hang up!'

'It's okay now, he's up in the city. Shoot.'

'Well, the word is that the hearing date for our court case is postponed again. Judge Jaris is out sick. Bad sick, I hear. They're bringing in a circuit judge from the Worcester area. We're re-scheduled for March 10th.'

'I don't see anything bad about that, Charlie. What's the problem?'

'The problem is that they're bringing in Judge Katherine Osmond. She's got a reputation as a hanging judge!'

'That doesn't sound too bad. Anything else?'

'Yes. My spies tell me that the Latimore Corporation has scheduled its heavy equipment for Eastboro, beginning on the fifteenth of March. Did you know that?'

'No I didn't, Charlie. I didn't marry the Corporation.' But you *thought* you did for a while there, didn't you, she lectured herself.

'Maybe you should have. Keep your powder dry!'

She had planned to confront him when he came home that night, but at three o'clock, when she was still diddling in their bedroom, her resolve began to weaken. It would be the first argument with her husband of three weeks. With her big husband. With her big bad tempered husband! Perhaps it would be better to wait for another time. *Probably* it would be better to wait!

She was still undecided at four thirty when she heard the Mercedes wheel into the drive. Caught only in her briefs, she hustled herself into a warm blue turtleneck sweater, a tartan wrap-around skirt, and hurried downstairs. He was waiting for her in the lounge, his favourite after-work Scotch in his hand. He passed her the half-glass of white wine that she preferred, and dropped into his easy chair with a groan of relief. She pulled up her floor-pillow beside his chair, as usual, and dropped on to it, her arms on his knees.

'You look beat, girl,' he probed. 'Something bothering?'

'I—not really,' she sighed, not wanting to burden him with her petty problems.

'Come on,' he coaxed. 'The truth, the whole truth—it's better that way.'

'I suppose,' she agreed, 'but you're tired, and——'

He wound one finger through her loose braid, and gave it a tiny tug. 'You'd better tell me,' he threatened.

'Yes, well,' she sighed again, struggling to escape his playful torment. 'I'm tired, Bruce. I think it's because I've got nothing to do. Jennie looked at me as if I were stealing her job this morning, and all I wanted to do was make up our bed. And every time I go into the kitchen Mrs Pemm reads me the riot act. I don't mean to complain, when you've got so many larger problems than mine. I am *trying* to adjust, but——'

'I know you're having trouble,' he said quietly. 'It was bound to happen. What should we do about it?'

'I—Bruce?' He bent down to her and kissed the top of her head. 'Bruce, if we could perhaps move back to the farm and then I could do for us without all this help around, and I know I could make you comfortable, and——'

He stopped her gently musical run of words by putting a finger across her lips. 'No,' he said. 'Too many ghosts live at Somerfield Farms.' She stopped immediately, eyes widened. 'We'll live in *my* house, Mary Kate. And after a while you'll have plenty to do, I'm sure. I meant to talk to you about the farm, but I thought we could wait for a month or so, when we'd both had a chance to settle into harness. But I guess it can't wait. I think we ought to sell the farmhouse, my dear.'

Things had become even worse than she had imagined. His face looked calm, but he had that 'I am the Master' look about him, and he surely meant for her to meekly agree. 'I—I can't do that,' she said, and flinched away as if she thought he would hit her.

'What the devil!' he asked. 'Why can't you sell it if I ask you to?'

'Because it's not mine,' she whispered. And you didn't ask me, you told me! She sat up stiffly. 'It belongs to Becky, not to me. The house and half of the farm belong to Becky. The other house, and the other half belong to Henry.'

'And you don't have any say in the matter? How did you expect to live after Becky married? You are Becky's guardian, aren't you?'

'I—I have a lifetime widow's pension from the Army. It's enough for me to live on. And yes, I'm Becky's guardian until she is eighteen.'

'Plenty of time,' he mused. 'The housing market is good now, even for a house that has to be moved. We'd better put it on the market.' He gulped the rest of his drink, as if the matter were closed. She sat very still, and tried to control her rising temper. He didn't understand, or he wouldn't understand!

'No,' she said firmly. 'I can't sell Becky's house.'

He had started to pick up the evening paper. His hands stopped in mid-motion. 'No?' he said, very softly. 'You mean you *won't* sell the house?'

She shook her head, and waited for the storm. It didn't come. Instead, he put both hands to her cheeks and gently kissed her imprisoned mouth. Then, as if nothing of importance had happened, he turned back to his newspaper. She sat up very straight, stiffened with determinate anger, then she tugged at the bottom of his newspaper. He lowered it enough so that she could see his face.

'I'm not going to let you make me do this,' she said

firmly. 'You can't make me do it.' And a pause. Then, in a more hesitant tone, 'Can you?' There was a tear struggling in the corner of her eye, he watched it escape and trail down her cheek.

'No,' he said calmly, 'apparently I can't make you do it.'

Dinner was a strained time that night, until Becky and Mattie both began teasing them for their solemnity, and eventually the evening broke clear of its storms, helped on by a generously portioned strawberry short cake. So, when at the top of the stairs, on their way to bed, he stopped. 'I almost forgot,' he said. 'There are a bunch of post-nuptial papers you have to sign. I want you to go up with me in the morning. Sanders, our Corporation Lawyer, will have them ready. Then you can join me in the board meeting, and we'll come home early.' There seemed to be nothing worth saying, and 'Yes my Lord' might have been just the tiniest bit servile. So she let it all pass, and enjoyed the evening, because the honeymoon was by no means over!

They left the house at eight thirty the next morning. It was a clear crisp day, with the thermometer hovering around the twenty degree mark, and a red sun poking up from the Atlantic Ocean a few miles to their east. He smiled at her as she came out of the house waving a piece of half-eaten toast in her hand. The encumbrance made it difficult for her to get into the bucket seat neatly. Her grey, knit skirt rode up high on her thigh, leaving a great deal of well-shaped leg on display. She gobbled at the toast, then looked for something to wipe the butter from her fingers. 'Don't hurry,' he chuckled, 'I like the view.'

'What? What's the matter?' she mumbled, struggling to swallow the rest of the toast.

'Nothing's the matter,' he returned. 'I was just thinking of building an addition to the house. A harem. You're too dangerous to be wandering loose around the world. You need to be put in purdah!'

'Well, I can't help it if your darn company starts things before I finish my breakfast,' she muttered. She had finally found a tissue in the glove compartment, and had pulled her skirt down to a more decorous level. 'What's that mean, *purdah*?'

'It means locked up, under guard, under close protection—especially from the males of the species.'

'Huh!' she ejaculated. 'All except you, I suppose. How ancient can you get! You're—you're nothing but a male chauvinist——'

'Pig?' he offered, starting the motor and moving them off.

'Oh, not pig,' she answered primly. 'I've been a farmer for all my life. I have a very great respect for pigs.'

'And that puts an end to this conversation, doesn't it,' he laughed. 'Until tonight, that is. You'll get yours, woman!'

'Promises, promises!' she returned.

This was her first daylight trip into the city with him. On her own, the trip would have been a polite method of hara kiri. She would usually sneak the Mustang in on one of the back streets, jostling for a place to double-park. And when she returned, nine times out of ten she would find herself penned in by a triple-parker. But Bruce calmly drove up in front of the Prudential building, stopped in the no parking zone, and stepped casually out on to the sidewalk while a waiting attendant took the car away to the underground parking garage.

'So that's how it is to be of the nobility,' she muttered as he clutched her arm and hurried her through the double-doors.

'Yes, that's how it is,' he laughed back at her. 'And now watch this.' He led her over to the bank of elevators, crowded at this time of day, except for one, which stood patiently waiting for him, it seemed. 'All a matter of executive privilege,' he told her solemnly.

'And a nice Christmas gift for the operator?' she teased.

'That too, witch.' On the fourteenth floor he handed her out. She followed him down a long narrow corridor, deep in golden dragon rugs. The offices were a mad house. He hurried her through a wide room which was wall-to-wall desks, all busy, and into an inner sanctum.

'Wait here.' He shoved her into an armchair settled in a corner by the thick windows.

'Story of my life,' she called after him. He turned around to glare at her. 'Yes *sir*! Wait here, *sir*!' she snapped. He grinned and disappeared through another door.

Ten minutes went by. She let her eyes wander around the room. For an office, it wasn't bad. Gold on the floors, light beige on the walls. Three prints hanging circumspectly between the windows. Copies of Dégàs, they looked to be. Four windows, closed against the March winds. A view out over the centre of the city. Two pigeons, risking their life in flight. Four traffic helicopters, jockeying for the best positions over the city's arteries, so that their radio stations would be the first with the traffic news. A typical Boston rush hour, and she was glad that she was fourteen storeys above it. A door opened behind her.

'Mrs Latimore?' The woman was middle-aged, well-kept, not a hair out of place. 'I'm Emma Raines, your husband's secretary. I'm sorry, but our Mr Sanders will be late. Your husband asks that you might come into the Board Room and watch the proceedings until the lawyer arrives?'

'Board meeting? I've never seen a real live board meeting,' Mary said. And you are just the kind of secretary that a very jealous new wife would love to have for her too-handsome husband, her eyes said. 'I've got such a lot to learn.'

'And so have we,' the secretary laughed, having read both messages.

They went out of the office arm in arm, down a small hall, and into a large conference room. Six men sat around a mahogany table. Six big men, she noticed. No ties. Every one of them wore construction boots. A working board. Bruce sat at the head of the table.

'Do I bow down or just curtsy,' Mary whispered to Emma from their position at the foot of the table. The secretary tugged her to one side and ushered her into a large comfortable swivel chair, built for the big men around the table. She climbed up into it with difficulty, her feet unable to touch the floor. When she tried to lean back, as the men were doing, the tensile springs refused to move under her tiny weight. 'Alice in Wonderland,' she muttered to Emma, who had settled beside her and whipped out a shorthand notebook.

'Gentlemen,' her husband was saying. 'This is Mary Kate, my wife. As of today she holds ten percent of the company stock. She looked down the table at him and raised her eyebrows. 'My wife is a specialist in—ah—agricultural construction,' he continued, with a wicked grin on his face. The men all turned to look at him. She stuck out her tongue at him, and tried to become invisible.

The meeting went right over her head. New projects, and the several foreign countries in which they were to be built. Completed projects, and a summary of their cost and profits. Make two million here, and lose a million there, and round everything off to the nearest hundred thousand dollars, she told herself. Her mind dreamed and her attention wandered, until gradually it impinged on her that there was an argument going on. The man in the middle was thumping on the table, and three of them were trying to talk at the same time. She heard the words, 'Route 695', and her antennae went up and her mind came to full battle stations.

'We've been working on this project for six years,' the man was complaining, 'and so far all we've collected is the partial payments on costs and direct expenses. We're carrying the load on interest payments, equipment leases, right-of-ways, everything. And the state is not going to pay us a penny of the profits until we get that damn mile finished. Six million dollars in profits! And if we don't get it soon, the interest we're paying on loans will have eaten the whole thing up. I think it's time to go down there and be—tough with that little lady.'

Her husband was on his feet, his face red. 'That's enough of that, Sandy,' he roared down the table. 'Route 695 is my own personal project, and I'll take care of it in my own way!'

'But hell, we can't let some sprig of a girl——'

'That's enough!'

Mary looked down the table at the complainer, to see his neighbour elbow him a couple of times and whisper in his ear. He shut up instantly and looked guardedly down the table to her. Emma tapped her on the arm. 'I think Mr Sanders must be here by now,' she said quietly. But Mary had seen out of the corner of her eye how her husband had been nodding his head at his secretary, and the message was easy to read. 'Get her out of here!' She went docilely.

It was another fifteen minutes before Sanders showed up. In the meantime Mrs Raines had furnished coffee, and disappeared, leaving Mary alone to think it all out. Last night it had been 'Sell the farmhouse'. Today it had been 'Ten per cent of the company stock'. Six million dollars profit, as soon as they finished that one mile of road through Somerfield Farms. Six million dollars? And 'It's my own project'. She shut it back into its own dark corner. Six million dollars. And then Tom Sanders arrived.

'In here, Mrs Latimore,' he urged, leading her into her husband's empty office. 'There are a number of routine things here that the boss wants you to sign, so if you'll just sit at his desk?'

It was the same story, of course. A chair designed for a big man, and refusing hospitality to a little woman who was obviously beneath its dignity. The lawyer set up a neat pile in front of her, and handed her a gold pen. 'I haven't used anything but a ball-point for years,' she apologised nervously. Why should I apologise to him? I'm the owner of stock. He's just an employee. Why am I shaking so?

'Right here and here, and here.' He was pointing to the appropriate blank spaces, his hand over the documents themselves. She sighed and signed her name. 'Mary Katherine Latimore.' It all looked so final. The reams of print, and then her little Palmer Method name. 'What's that—what's that for?' she stammered. He whipped the first set of papers off the pile.

'Nothing much,' he said. 'That's your receipt for the shares, and your proxy for your husband to vote them.'

'You mean I don't get to vote?'

'Of course not,' he laughed, 'but you do get the dividends, you know.'

She shook her head, trying to clear her brain. Lordy, I wish I had stayed at the farm with the chickens, she sighed to herself.

'And here, and also here,' he continued. She scribbled her name this time, in self defence. Maybe they can't prove I signed it, she told herself. She looked up at the lawyer again. 'Those are shares of the company stock in the name of Mr Latimore's new daughter. Rebecca, is it?'

'And the proxy, so Mr Latimore can vote it?'

'Yes, as usual.' But wasn't that nice? He had no need to do that. Becky didn't really need the money. Not now, at any rate, but she would be thrilled to hear what her new father had done! Mary relaxed, leaned back in the chair, and it yielded slightly to her weight. 'Anything else?' she asked, at peace with the world.

'Oh yes,' the lawyer said. 'Here and here please.' This document was printed on legal-size paper, and a word or two caught her eye. She stopped to read. An application to the Superior Court of the Commonwealth of Massachusetts, for the adoption of Rebecca Elizabeth Chase, a minor, in joint custody with Bruce P. Latimore, the plea being entered by Mary Katherine Chase, aka Mrs Mary Katherine Latimore. It stuck just the right note. She laughed as she carefully inscribed her name at the bottom of each of the six copies. What a thing to think of! What a wonderful thing to think of! And attached to it, in his bold print, was a note. 'Mary Kate,' it said, 'Becky and I thought this would be a nice present to you.' She folded up the note and pressed it against her cheek before sliding it into the outer pocket of her jacket.

'And just one more, Mrs Latimore.'

'Of course,' she sighed happily. What a wonderful man she had married. What a—she had already signed her first name to the last document before the word caught her eye. This too was printed in legal-size stationery. And the word that had caught her eye, at the top, was 'Quitclaim'. She stopped and carefully put the pen down on the desk. 'Mr Sanders,' she said quietly, 'what was my—husband's instruction about this one?'

'He said you were to sign it, Mrs Latimore.'

She nodded, winking a tear out of her eye as she read. Her hand moved towards the pen again, but did not pick it up. *Quitclaim!* The respondent, Mary Katherine Latimore, aka Mary Katherine Chase, requests permission of the court to withdraw her opposition to case docketed 19872, in the matter of the construction of certain roadways by the Latimore Construction Corporation.

'He wanted me to sign it?' she repeated, sounding as miserable as she felt.

'He said most especially that one,' the lawyer

returned. Of course, most especially that one. Six million dollars of profit. Love, honour, and obey. Henry's cows, and Becky's farm, and the promises she had made to the Colonel as he lay on his death bed. That's what I'm worth. Me and Becky and Henry and Anna, and all the farm. Six million dollars. If you can't beat them, join them! And all the black ravening beasts in her mind burst their bonds and came roaring up to her centres of attention. Why did he marry me? Why me? Mattie could have had plenty of tutors. He had plenty of society girls to fill his bed. Why did he marry me, a nobody? A little farm girl who had nothing he wanted—except a mile of road!

He married me for a mile of road! And he's sitting in there expecting me to sign it all away! We'll adopt Becky, and he'll have me in his bed for the fun of it every night. Until the road gets built. And then what? He's already bought me, with ten percent of his rotten stock. And I promised to love, honour, and cherish him. And I promised to obey him!

Tears were streaming down both cheeks, and she had nothing to dry them with. She looked up hopelessly at the lawyer. He tried to avoid her eyes. Her hand was on the pen. All she had to do was to pick it up, and finish writing her name. All the contests would be over. She would live just this side of heaven—until he got his road built. And Becky and Henry and Anna would——

She picked up the pen, looked without seeing at the paper before her. And then, with large wild strokes, she wrote 'NO!' all across its face and the signature line. She pushed back the chair and managed to stand on weak and trembling legs. Stiff legged she stalked to the door and went through it.

'Mrs Latimore,' the lawyer called after her. She passed Emma's desk in a blur of tears, snatching at her purse as she did so. As she came to the outer door, Emma came in from the conference room. 'Mrs

Latimore!' she called after Mary's retreating back. She stalked down the corridor, ignoring the flooding tears. The private elevator was waiting, door open. The young girl operator noticed the tears. 'Mrs Latimore?' she asked. Mary paid no attention. When they reached the lobby she turned around in a circle once, to savour it all, then she pulled her shoulders back and marched out into the street.

CHAPTER NINE

ANNA was in the kitchen when she heard the cab pull up outside the house. It was unusual enough to bring her to the side window. She watched for only a second as the tiny figure of her mother-in-law stumbled out of the car and wavered up the rock-paved path. Without really thinking about it, Anna pushed the alarm button on the intercom set that connected the house to the barn. When one of the farm hands answered, she blurted out, 'Find Henry. Get him up to the house. Quick!' Then she ran for the front door.

She was back in the kitchen twenty minutes later, holding the back door half open, when Henry came up the path from the barn at full speed. 'What?' he gasped. 'You all right?'

She grabbed him by the forearm and pushed him towards the parlour. 'It's Ma,' she said softly, hoping not to be overheard. 'She won't say a word. She's just sitting in the rocking chair, rocking back and forth. I've given her a cup of coffee, but she hasn't drunk it. She's just sitting there, looking like death warmed over. You go in. I'd better stay out of the way. Leave the doors open. I want to hear.' She pushed him ahead of her, out into the tiny hall that interconnected the rooms.

He stopped just outside the parlour door, in a position where he could see in, but could not be seen. His stepmother was rocking back and forth in the low rocker, her face straight ahead, and as pale as death. Her arms gripped the chair so hard that her fingers were turning blue at the ends. She hardly seemed to blink as she rocked, back and forth. He shrugged himself more neatly into his shirt, took a big breath, plastered a smile on his face, and ambled into the room.

'Hi Ma,' he said cheerfully. 'What brings you among the country folk at this hour of the day?'

She stopped rocking, looked up at him as if he were a stranger, and pushed herself up out of the chair. 'Henry,' she said in a high strained voice, 'he wanted to trade me for a mile of road. I've left him.' It was a matter-of-fact statement, as if she were commenting on the weather. A crash from the kitchen, where Anna had just dropped two plates, drew his attention away for barely a second. When he looked back the tiny figure was slowly collapsing towards the floor.

'Anna,' he yelled. 'Come!' He knelt down beside the crumpled body. She was breathing shallowly, her eyes closed, and her lipstick glared out from the middle of a colourless face. Anna hurried in behind him, and knelt. He picked up one of Mary's tiny hands and began chafing it, trying to restore circulation. He felt helpless. This was the woman who had stabilised their lives, brought the Colonel up out of his grief, reorganised the farm, led them into the future.

'I never realised how small she is,' he whispered to his wife.

'Put her up on the couch,' Anna told him, 'then call the doctor.'

'The doctor won't come,' he replied bitterly. 'They don't make house calls any more.'

It was Anna's cachet of smelling salts that brought her around. She sat up, unwilling to remain supine, and sipped at the hot tea that Anna had prepared. Henry fussed around her, arranging pillows, stretching a blanket over her, touching up her eyes with his huge handkerchief, until she regained control. 'Don't fuss,' she commanded him, with almost a touch of her normal tone. He came around to the front of the couch and knelt down in front of her.

'I'm going to go over and pound him into the ground like a fence post,' he told her. 'What did he do? Did he hit you?'

She took his wrist in both her hands. 'No,' she sighed, 'nothing like that. Everything is sophistication in the Latimore Corporation. That one mile of road is worth six million dollars in profit to him. I guess he figured it was worth it to marry me. I suspect he planned to divorce me at some suitable time after he gets his road built. I never realised—it never crossed my mind. I guess he was right in the end, wasn't he. While I was defending the front gate he sneaked in the back door, and did he ever clobber this country girl.'

'Don't say that, Ma,' he responded. 'You're the smartest girl in town. I'd better go punch the bastard.' He made to get up, but she held the corner of his shirt sleeve.

'No, don't, Henry.' The words seemed to come softly down on the wind from distant pine trees. But then why not, she asked herself. Maybe Henry, at least could get some relief by a physical punch-out. But she knew why. She loved Henry, who was as big as Bruce, but not as ruthless. He might get hurt. Or Bruce might get hurt. And she loved *him*, too. It's surely strange she thought. How can you love and hate a man all at the same time?

'All right,' Henry said. 'As usual, you're the boss. Drink more tea. What do you want us to do? Shall I bring the girls over here?'

Mary sipped at the tea again, feeling its warmth for the first time, savouring of the leaf, reflecting. When she set the cup down on the waiting saucer she had her battle-plan ready.

'Henry, the court hearing is tomorrow. The girls will be okay for a day or two, until both our tempers cool. You'll put me up for a while?'

'Of course, Ma,' Anna answered. Which was only proper. She was the woman of the house, and New

England traditions change very slowly. Mary flashed them both a thankful smile. And then another thought came, and she nibbled her lip.

'He might come after me,' she said softly. 'There aren't too many places to look, and he wants his road badly.'

'Let him come,' Henry snorted. 'I thought he was a nice guy! If he shows up around here he'll get a knuckle sandwich.'

'I—I don't want you to fight,' she counselled. 'There's no sense in aggravating the situation. I *do* have to go back to him—if he wants me. But I need a few days. Just a few days.'

'You don't have to go back to him,' Henry snapped. 'He's only using you!'

'I *do* have to,' she replied firmly. 'I made him promises. In church, and in my heart. I have to keep them, no matter what he does.'

'Okay,' her step-son muttered. 'I don't see it, but if that's the way you want it. And now we'd better get you upstairs and into bed.

'I'm all right,' Mary said. 'All I need is a little comfort and a little rest. Help me up to my feet.'

'Help you hell!' Henry snapped. 'At least I can boss *you* around.' He swept her up in his arms and carried her up the narrow stairs to the bedroom, where she dozed for an hour, surrounded by one of Anna's flannel nightgowns, and a houseful of love.

Latimore came at three thirty, after both girls had returned from school. Henry must have been waiting, because Mary heard both their voices out in front of the house, just under her window.

'Is she here?' Bruce asked. It was like the opening statement in a formal duel, where both sides touch sabres before they begin.

'She's here,' Henry replied coldly. He made no attempt to amplify his statement.

'I want her now! She's my wife.'

'She happens to be my mother. What did you do to her, you bastard! I've known her all her life, and I've never seen her like this before.'

'It was a misunderstanding. Let me by, I've got to talk to her.'

'She doesn't want to talk to you. And don't try to push me around, Latimore. She collapsed, damn you. Right in the middle of my floor. What the hell did you do to her?'

'It's a misunderstanding, I tell you. I have to see her.'

'Misunderstanding? That sent her careening around the countryside like a ghost ship? Let me tell you straight. You don't come in. Not until she says so. And she's not saying. She's still asleep—unconscious.'

'Oh my God. I have to——'

'Oh my God is right. Try a little prayer. And get your hand off my arm!'

'I have to see her. I could fight my way in. You're not all that tough.'

'We'll never know until you try, will we?' Henry answered. 'And if you try that and get by me, you'll have Anna to contend with. And just suppose you get by both of us, where would that leave you with her?'

'Damn you, Chase. Damn you!'

'And damn you too, Latimore. We were a happy family until you broke your way in. And all for a lousy road. She thinks you married her for a lousy mile of road. Did you know that?'

'I—yes, I know.'

'Then why don't you just get out of here. I'll call the girls after a while and arrange something for them.'

'Ask her to call me, Henry. Please. I have to know how she is, and what she wants me to do.'

'I'll tell her. I don't think she'll call. Good-bye.'

'I—don't forget, Henry.'

'I'm not likely to forget. Not after what you've done

to Ma. And I'd prefer you to call me Mr Chase. Good-bye.'

Mary was up early the next morning. Early enough to call the house before the girls went off to school. Becky answered the telephone, and Mattie joined her on the extension. She hardly knew where to begin, but the girls must know, and have their choice. Mattie inadvertently made it easier.

'Daddy said that you and him had a mad on,' she chirped in her light happy voice. 'He said married grown-ups have that sometimes.'

'That's true, my dears,' she said. 'I have to be away for a few days, then I'll come back.'

'Oh me, that's a relief,' Becky commented. 'Pop said you were so mad at him you might not. You *are* coming back?'

'Yes dear. In a few days. Will you both be all right where you are?'

'We'll be okay, Ma,' Becky returned. 'I'll watch after the little terror, here.'

'Don't say it like that,' Mattie objected. 'Sweet little terror—that's what daddy says.'

'Okay, sweet little terror,' Becky accepted drily. 'But you're sure you're okay, Ma? If you decide to not come back, I'm coming to you, you know.'

'Me too,' Mattie added. 'We're gonna miss the school bus!'

'Going to,' Becky corrected. 'Going to, not gonna. Hey Ma? I got my driver's permit yesterday. Pop went down with me. What a difference it makes when they know a man is with you!'

The phrase was still running around in her head when Anna coaxed her down to breakfast. And of course they do, she told herself. It's a man's world. They all notice the difference when your man is with you!

She managed to finish both halves of the piece of toast, and two cups of black coffee, with Anna threatening dire destruction if she should leave a crust. When the telephone rang, she knew it must be him. 'You answer it, Anna,' she pleaded. 'I don't want to talk to him. Not yet.'

It wasn't *him*. The scratchy female voice at the other end identified herself as Charles Momson's secretary. 'You mean tomorrow,' Mary gasped, after listening briefly.

'Yes, tomorrow. And Mr Momson is in the Veterans Administration Hospital in Brockton!'

'I don't understand,' Mary stammered.

'None of us do. Her name is Osmond, Judge Katherine Osmond. She lined up both sides in the case this morning and raised holy hell. She said evidently Judge Jaris had made a career out of this case, but she was going to settle it. Poor Charlie immediately felt bad, and had to go to the hospital. But the Judge says it doesn't matter. Both principals are to be in the court in New Bedford tomorrow for a Bench conference. Nine o'clock. Be prompt!'

'Okay, I understand,' Mary sighed. 'I'll be there. How's Charlie?'

'Outside of a bad cold and a weak backbone, he's fine. The chief surgeon at the hospital is an old friend, you know.'

'Trouble, Ma?' Anna asked as Mary put the phone down very slowly.

'No more than usual,' she responded. 'It's a case of rats and sinking ships. It'll come out alright.'

Mary was not all that confident the next morning when she wheeled Henry's truck into the only available parking spot outside the Superior Court in New Bedford. There was a 'reserved' sign on the parking space. 'Reserved for Judge Jaris.' And to the devil with you, Judge, she snorted under her breath as she cut across the lawn. The building smelled musty, left over. 'Lizzie Borden went on trial here for axe murder,' she reminded herself, and felt a little better. After all, Lizzie had been found not guilty!

Upstairs in the smaller chamber of the court Judge Katherine Osmond shrugged into her robes, smoothed them affectionately around her sixty-year-old frame, and took a quick peek in the mirror. It was hard enough to have to come down from Worcester, only to find that the city had no hotel. She had ended up in a motel on the bridge, where the low-tide smells and the lack of her kind of coffee, had put her on edge for the day. She patted her blue-white hair into place and marched out into the courtroom, where the bailiff was already sounding the 'Oyez, Oyez.' She settled herself into her chair, and looked around the well of the court.

Only two things upset her normally fair-handed approach to the law. One was domineering men, and the other was tardiness. And here at the first case of the day she found both. The big man with the beetling eyebrows sitting at the plaintiff's table looked as if he had come off an FBI 'Most Wanted' poster. The respondent's table was empty. And then down the side aisle there was a clatter, and a tiny girl, looking hardly more than eighteen, came stumbling through the knots of spectators, her arms full of documents. Judge Katherine Osmond sighed. It was obviously going to be one of those days. The late party scrambled up to her place, scattered her papers on the table, and plumped into a chair, exhausted. The clerk called the case. Somerfield Farms versus Latimore Construction. The Judge had hardly slept a wink the previous night, and had not been able to read the briefs, the summaries of past court action in the case. She gavelled the court to attention.

'Now as I understand it,' the Judge started to say, and then stopped. What in heaven's name was the man up to? The big man. He had been talking to his lawyer when the girl came in, and the noise attracted his attention. He got up from his chair and rumbled across the room like a tank on manoeuvres. The little girl got up from her chair and backed up against the wall, her face contorted with fear. The Judge rapped her gavel again. 'You there—Mr—whatever your name is, will you please——'

'Mary Kate, I have to talk to you before this nonsense begins,' he roared at the little girl.

'Get him away from me,' the girl screamed. 'Get him away from me. Don't you dare lay a hand on me! Oh God, why isn't there a policeman around when you need one!'

'All right you—Mr—whoever,' the Judge snapped. 'Back to your seat. Bailiff, put that man back where he belongs!' She banged her gavel a couple more times. The five foot six inch bailiff was doing his best, squeezing between the girl and the six foot man. 'You there, sit down!' the Judge demanded. The man looked up at her. 'I have to talk to her,' he stated flatly.

'Well do it on your own time,' the Judge snapped. A pair of state troopers had just entered the court. She signalled for help, and they ran down the aisle. The big man noted the reinforcements, muttered something under his breath, and went back to his own table.

'Later, Mary Kate,' he said ominously.

'Any later than this, young man,' Judge Katherine snapped, 'and I'll have you up for contempt of court. Sit down. Shut up.' There was temporary order in the court. 'Now then,' she continued, 'is the plaintiff represented?'

The other man at the table got up. 'Yes, your honour,' he said. 'The Latimore Corporation is represented by the chairman of the board, Mr Bruce Latimore.'

'Bruce Latimore,' the Judge repeated. Big man. And the name didn't sound too good. Surly looking fellow. Wish I had a cup of real coffee. 'You there, you're not the same lawyer that was here yesterday?'

'Of course he isn't,' Latimore interjected. 'I fired that jackass yesterday. Damn lawyers!'

The Judge snapped her gavel twice on the little sounding board. 'Watch your language, Mr Latimore,' she warned. 'And the Respondent? Are you a lawyer, little girl?'

'No, I'm not,' the girl said. A soft but distinct contralto. Not so young as she first appeared. If only she could do something with that mass of hair. Ah well. Judge Katherine sighed for what might have been, and memories coloured her voice, took away the harshness, added a little sympathy. 'Then what are you, girl?'

'I'm the Respondent,' the girl said. 'Somerfield Farms. I'm the president of the company. My—my name is Mary Kate Latimore.'

'No lawyer, Miss Latimore?'

'That's Mrs Latimore, your honour. My lawyer was stricken in court ˙yesterday. He's in the Veterans Hospital, and I can't afford to hire another one.'

'And you think you can get by without legal counsel?'

'I—I guess I have to, your honour.'

'All right, Mrs Latimore,' the Judge returned. 'The court will do its best to guard your interests. Mrs Latimore, hey? Are you perhaps related to the—to Mr Latimore over there?'

'She's my wife, your honour,' Bruce interrupted.

The judge whacked the gavel again. 'I think the girl can speak for herself,' she lectured him. He glared back at her.

'Now, in the interest of saving time, Mrs Latimore, suppose you explain your position. Keep it simple.'

'Easy enough for you to say,' Mary whispered under her breath. All you have to do is sit up there and bang the gavel. And I have to stand here like some stupid cow, with him glowering at me!

'Sometime before noon,' the Judge prodded. 'I do have a luncheon engagement.' The touch of sarcasm cut through the morass in Mary's mind. She snapped her eyes away from the other table, not more than six feet from her, and began a short and precise statement about the road, its alternatives, and the problems it caused for the farm. She had brought along with her two large sketches of the proposed road and its alternative. The Judge looked interested. As Mary turned away from the Bench for another paper she was surprised to see that the courtroom was rapidly filling up. A number of people were scribbling in notebooks. Three photographers were lurking near the rear door. What in God's world attracted *them*, she wondered, as she picked up her next exhibit.

'And you, Mr Latimore,' the Judge interjected, 'do you have anything to say so far?'

'You bet I have, your honour,' he grated. He scraped back his chair and came out before the Bench, hardly a foot from where Mary was standing. He glowered at her. 'As usual,' he told the Judge, 'the little lady has got it all wrong. Why they ever let women in law courts I'll never understand, but——' The gavel pounded him to silence.

'It's obvious that you practise a deal of chauvinism in your organisation, Mr Latimore,' the Judge said softly, 'but your generalities are not making you too popular with the two women in *this* court. I think you'd better sit down.'

'Damn it, your honour,' he growled. 'Can't you see that she's just a crazy mixed up kid? What she needs is a good——'

Whatever it was he thought she needed, Mary was not prepared to find out. As he turned and reached out a hand at her she fumbled backwards around the table and vaulted over the low rail that separated the well of the court from the spectator seats. She stood on the other side, both hands on the rail, trembling like a fawn in flight. 'Please,' she begged, 'please don't let him get his hands on me.'

'Oh, he's one of that type,' the Judge snorted. 'Bailiff, sit that man down and keep him down!' There was another few minutes of confusion, then the gavel rapped again.

'Come back up here,' the Judge gestured. Mary hesitantly walked around to the swinging gate and approached the Bench. 'Just to satisfy my curiosity,' the Judge said, 'tell me how long you two have been married.'

'Three——' Mary stuttered, watching him out of the corner of her eye. He was pounding the table in front of him with his fist. 'Three weeks,' she hurried to say.

'Three weeks? And you've come to this already? I wish it were germane to this case. I'd really like to hear what's going on.'

'It is—germane, I mean!' The words came rushing out, without control. 'He wanted the road. One mile of road. That's what he wanted, and he couldn't get it, so he married me and then tried to make me file a quitclaim for this case and I wouldn't do it and now he's terribly mad at me and I'm scared he'll—I'm scared. I don't know why, I'm just scared!'

'And is that true, Mr Latimore? You tried to make her file a quitclaim in this case?' The Judge's voice had gone up one octave, and she held the gavel as if its next whack would be on the top of his head.

'Hell no, that's not true,' he stated firmly. He stood up again. Mary shrank back against the panelling of the Bench. 'His lawyer,' she cried. 'Make him tell about his lawyer!'

'So my lawyer did bring her a quitclaim,' he agreed. There was injury written in every syllable, and the heavy eyelids looked as if the eagles were about to strike. 'So that's why I fired the stupid clod. Heaven protect me from *all* lawyers!'

'You may need Heaven indeed,' Judge Osmond commented quietly. 'All right young lady, is there anything else you want me to consider about this case?'

'Yes sir—ma'am. Yes your honour,' she stumbled. 'There are some things. My lawyers wrote two of them up as submissions. May I tell you about them?'

'Indeed you may,' the Judge agreed. 'And while you're doing that the bailiff will send out and get us a cup of coffee. Would that make you feel better?'

Mary Kate managed to wipe the tears from her eyes and catch her breath, and then she began. 'The first problem is the cemetery,' she began.

'What cemetery!' He was on his feet again. The gavel banged twice.

'Sit that man down!' the Judge barked. 'All right my dear, what about the cemetery?'

'It's—your honour should know that where our farm is located was once the centre of Eastboro. But back in, oh, 1800 or so, the new highway from Boston to New Bedford went to the east of us, and so the whole town moved down to where it is now. But they left the cemetery behind. And if the road comes on to our farm it will go right through the cemetery.'

'Ah,' the Judge chuckled. 'And of course the law of the Commonwealth prohibits such a taking. Did you know that, young lady?'

'I—yes, your honour, I knew that, and I thought——'

'She never had a straight thought in her life,' he roared. 'And all along I thought it was that town drunk that you maintained as a lawyer! You've thought all of this up by yourself, haven't you, Mary Kate?' He grabbed her by the shoulders and shook her back and forth, until it seemed that her neck might snap. The Judge's gavel was hammering like a machine gun, the bailiff was vainly trying to recover his balance, and the Judge was jibbering like a person gone mad. He stopped shaking her. 'You deserved that, Mary Kate,' he told her.

'Your honour,' he addressed the court again. 'This has come as some surprise, but——'

'I can see it has,' the Judge said grimly. 'That will be five hundred dollars. I hold you in contempt of court, Mr Latimore. Are you all right, Mrs Latimore?'

Mary Kate nodded assent from her position leaning against the corner of the respondent's table. Her face was pale.

He shrugged aside the Judge's threat as if it meant nothing. Which is probably true, Mary told herself. What's five hundred dollars to him? Her shoulders ached where his huge hands had dug in almost to the bone. She stretched her neck to relieve some of the tension. Her head was beginning to ache.

'But as I recall,' Bruce continued, 'the law states that where public good is involved, a cemetery can be moved, providing the families of all those buried there are properly notified. My men will get on that at once. Do you have something else up your deceiving little sleeve, Mary Kate?' He looked so stern. So—patriarchal. And I love him, she told herself. If he gets a chance he'll surely murder me. Surely.

'It won't be all that easy,' she told him softly. 'The last interment was on June 15, 1826. And one of the people buried there was Peamaquot, the War Chief of the Wampanoag Indian tribe. He was buried there in 1686, and I believe his family might be quite scattered. Not to mention Tobias Black. He was a freedman who fought in the Gloucester Regiment during the Revolution. His family may still be in Africa, and then——'

'The whole thing is an argument in a rain barrel,' he roared at her. She shrank away from him, but stiffened her spine, determined not to run away.

'I'll be the judge of that,' Judge Osmond said. 'Is there anything else, Mary Kate? I may call you that?'

'Yes—yes of course,' Mary replied. 'On the other side of our farm—on the west side. Last year we invited some archaeological students in from the University of

Massachusetts, and they found these.' She spilled out
an envelope of arrowheads, and bone awls. 'They think
that a major Indian settlement may have been located
in that area. The University has expressed a formal
interest, and I thought——'

The judge was wearing a broad smile now. 'You
thought that the law prohibiting disturbance of known
artifact areas until they have first been completely
explored—you thought that law might possibly apply?'

'I thought—perhaps?' Mary stuttered. She was
beginning to develop a great fondness for this white-
haired minister of justice!

'And have you a submission about this?' Mary
nodded and handed up the second package of
documents.

'Damn it all,' Bruce roared, 'it doesn't amount to a
hill of beans, your honour. I tell you——'

'You'd better not tell me anything at this moment,'
the Judge said. 'You are about two steps from a great
deal of trouble, Mr Latimore. Now then, Mary Kate,
do you have some other item you wanted recognised?'

'Perhaps it isn't important,' Mary responded. 'It was
just brought to my attention today.' From her purse she
pulled two copies of a colour photograph which had
been sent to her by the team of naturalists who had
explored Selby Brook.

'What's this?' The Judge picked up the two pictures.
'A frog?'

'Yes, your honour, a frog.' She passed up the letter
which had accompanied the pictures. 'This frog was
found in the swamp on our farm. The letter says that it
is not identifiable among any of the species of frogs
listed in the United States.'

The Judge put down the papers and laughed until her
sides shook. 'Oh Lord, Mary Kate,' she gasped. 'The
snail-darter syndrome!' The Judge was laughing so
much she had tears in her eyes. When she finally cleared

them, still chuckling, she said, 'Do you know what this means, Mr Latimore?'

'No I don't!' he grumbled. 'And it doesn't make a penny's worth of difference. I could settle the whole thing if you'd give me a minute to explain!' The gavel hit the pad again.

'You'll get your turn later,' the Judge said. 'Your wife should have been a lawyer, Mr Latimore.'

His mouth snapped in Mary's direction, and his eyes narrowed. 'Maybe she should,' he said sombrely. 'What does the frog mean?'

'Last year the Supreme Court of the United States had a case involving a very large dam, and a very small fish. The dam was almost complete, ready to be put in service, when it was proved that if it were closed, the snail darters who lived nowhere else in the world, would be exterminated. The Court ruled that the dam was not to be completed. And your wife, Mr Latimore, has discovered a new species of swamp frog!'

'Your honour!' His voice would jar the earthquake-measuring machinery in Boston Mary thought, and he's getting madder and madder and—Oh God, what am I going to do? 'Your honour,' he repeated, 'this is all a tempest in a teacup. I can assure you that nothing the Latimore Corporation is doing could affect any of these things—especially the damn frog!'

'Nothing except Becky's house and Henry's farm and my whole life!' She stood toe to toe with him and glared back at him. She could actually *see* him losing his temper. First the furrows on his forehead wrinkled. Then his nose twitched, and the left side of his mouth began to vibrate, and his face began to mottle with purple. She watched it all in slow motion, knowing she was in danger, unable to run.

'Damn you, Mary Kate,' he roared. 'It's just a great big game with you, isn't it. You've gone to all these lengths just so those damn reporters can plaster us all over the papers, haven't you!'

She was stunned by his unjust accusation, but when she glanced back into the depths of the court room she could see the smiling faces of at least a dozen reporters, and although cameras were prohibited by law, there was a crowd of cameramen standing by the back door. Nevertheless, she felt, it was so cruel, this accusation, so cruel. She turned back to him and told him so, and watched as he completely went to pieces. His heavy hands landed on her shoulders again, and her head rocked back and forth like a dory in a wild, wild sea. All chance to think had fled. She could not even hear clearly what he was muttering. Nor could she hear the slam of the gavel or the shrill call of the Judge. He was still rattling her around when other hands grabbed him and pulled him away.

Mary Kate had lost all sense of time or place. It was all replaced by fear. As soon as she felt the release from his hands her body jumped back without directions. She lost one sandal in the doing. One hand wiped at her tears, trying to clear her vision, and then she turned and ran. Through the little gate, down the corridor alongside the seats, where the reporters followed her every move, through the double doors, where the sun seemed to beckon protectively, and out.

Behind her she could hear Bruce's feet pounding after her. Oh God, she thought, this is really it. He's going to kill me now! But there was a second clash at the door behind her. She looked back just in time to see two policemen knock him down with a gang tackle, and drag him back into the court. Camera flashbulbs were flashing in her face, distorting her vision even further. Wearily, she staggered over to Henry's truck, tore off the parking ticket in disgust, waited just long enough to catch her breath and clear her eyes, and drove off. All of which, of course, made her miss the best court room scene of the day.

CHAPTER TEN

'Oh it was terrible,' she recounted that night over the supper table. 'I felt like a fool! I thought sure he was going to hit me. He was so angry! And his face turned all red and his cheeks puffed out, and he shook me so hard I think all my brains came loose. 'I'm lucky he didn't catch me on the way out!'

'Catch you?' Anna looked surprised. 'I heard on the radio that—oh dear, I was making biscuits!' She jumped up and ran out of the room. Henry denied any knowledge of the radio broadcast, 'Because we've had an overall drop of two percent in our cream output this month,' he said, 'and I'm not at all sure yet that those sections of Guyana hybrid corn are holding true.'

Her mind was readjusting to accept the new subject, when the telephone rang.

'Ma?' It was Becky calling. 'He's not coming home tonight, Ma. I wouldn't bother, but Mattie's upset. I think she needs you.'

'But—it's seven o'clock, Becky. We left the court house before noontime!'

'You left, Ma. You left. It was on all the television at six o'clock. They had a picture of you shaking your fist at him, and running down the hall and out of the court house. Boy was that funny.'

'Well you've got a very funny idea of funny, Missy,' she said, her voice revealing all the misery that she felt. 'All right, I'll come over for a while. But if he's there, I—I can't stay, Becky. I think he wants to murder me, or something.'

'Of course he won't be here,' Becky assured her. There was something about the way she said it that

167

caused Mary Kate to stop and think. Of course he won't be there? As if it were something she was absolutely sure of? And then it struck her. After that horrible display in the courtroom, he would have gone back to his friends in Boston, back to someplace where he was appreciated! But in any event, if Mattie needed her—'I'll be right over,' she told Becky.

Despite all her new-found determination, she sat outside the house for ten minutes or more after she arrived, working up her nerve, checking for his car, or any of his possessions—any of his *other* possessions, she quickly corrected herself.

Mattie was very upset. She missed her father mightily, and it took many minutes for Mary to soothe her battered spirit. By nine o'clock, with Mattie now calm and ready for bed, Mary decided to leave Becky to her own devices, and went off to bed with the younger girl. 'I'll just share the twin bed in your room, shall I?' she asked the child.

'Wonderful, Ma! And would you tell me a make-up story like you did before?' They shut themselves off from the world, up in the third-floor turret room, and by ten o'clock Mattie was asleep. But her new mother tossed and turned throughout the night, not dropping off to sleep until the dawn sun was already fingering the eastern windows.

It was eleven o'clock in the morning when Mrs Pemm knocked on the door and came in. 'I had a terrible time finding you, Mrs Latimore,' the cook panted. 'I looked in every bedroom in the house.' The exertion, the steps, and the message had driven her to the point where she could hardly breathe. 'It's the telephone. He wants you. And he says you'd better hurry.'

He wants you! Better hurry! The words brought her up out of the bed with startling speed. She snatched up her green terrycloth robe and slid it over her shortie nightgown, and was running down the stairs before she had quite opened her eyes. Only to find that it was the wrong man!

'Charlie Momson,' she snarled at him. 'After that fiasco yesterday I could kill you!'

'Simmer down, Mz Mary,' the old man replied. 'You've done my health a world of good already. I'm at the office. It was twenty-four-hour flu, or something.'

'I know it wasn't flu,' she snapped at him. 'It was more like yellow jaundice, you darn coward!'

'Call it what you will,' he laughed. 'At my age I have to protect my nerves. What are you going to do?'

'Me? What am *I* going to do? Well, the first thing is I'm going to go out and try to hire a lawyer who doesn't run at the sight of a tough judge, that's what!'

'Now now, Mary Kate,' he returned, 'there's no need for that kind of talk. I'm still representing you. In fact I have been called to the court today about your case. That wasn't what I meant. I meant what are you going to do about him?'

'About him? You should have been there, Charlie. I thought he was going to murder me right there in the court room. I think that the only thing I can do is to keep out of his way. To run away someplace. To hide until this whole affair blows over. Charlie? Why are you laughing like that? Charlie?'

It took some little time for the lawyer to calm down. And when he did, all he said was 'You'd better read the morning papers, Mary Kate!'

She wandered out into the kitchen, a very confused woman. She accepted the coffee mug that Mrs Pemm handed to her, and then sat down at the table. 'Did the girls get off to school okay?' she asked.

'They did,' the cook replied. 'Although I had to drive them out with my broom. They were so tied up with the paper, and giggling, and all. What are you going to do?'

'Do about what?' she sighed.

'Him. The papers. The television. The radio. Haven't you heard anything?'

'I guess not,' she sighed. 'The papers? Where are they?'

'On the table in front of you. You made the front page in both Boston papers, and one Providence paper.'

'O Lord protect me,' Mary Kate prayed. 'He was mad enough when I saw him in court, now if he finds out he's in the newspapers, he'll really let me have it.' She scooped the mass of newsprint up and jiggled it into a single pile. The *Boston Herald*, a tabloid scandal sheet, was on top.

'Will She or Won't She?' the big black headlines read; and down below it, covering half the page, was a picture of Mary Kate Latimore, running down the front steps of the court house, with only one shoe on. A clever artist had drawn in over the photograph a big black key, which seemingly she held in her left hand. And then underneath the picture, the story:

'World famous construction boss and man-about-town Bruce Latimore is vacationing in New Bedford this week, deeply concerned about the reactions of his newly-wed wife. Jailed for contempt of court yesterday, Latimore was informed by Judge Katherine Osmond that he would remain in the Slammer until wife Mary Kate Latimore sees fit to sign his release. At this time lovely Mary Kate is playing hard to find. This latest adventure in Latimore's woman-starred career would seem to leave the giant Construction Company headless for some time to come. Mary Kate, will you or won't you?'

She was too startled to cry, and too fearful to laugh. All she could manage was a fretful 'Oh my!' repeated over and over again. Mrs Pemm came around the table and looked over her shoulder. 'Nice picture,' she commented. Mary's startled eyes shifted back to the photograph. 'He's going to kill me,' she said morosely.

'Probably,' Mrs Pemm contributed. 'You want eggs for breakfast?'

Mary shook her head. No eggs. No ham. No nothing. Was this how Marie Antoinette felt on the morning they took her to the guillotine? She was numb, absolutely numb. Her brain refused to function. For one moment all thought about the road had vanished from her mind. Only one thought ran through her brain. Bruce is in jail, and I put him there! And sitting here moping won't make a bean's worth of difference. Wearily she pulled herself back into shape and went out to the telephone. Charlie Momson answered on the fifth ring.

'I was halfway out the door,' he said. 'I've been called by the clerk of the court to come in for a decision by Judge Osmond. Something's coming down, Mary Kate. What can I do for you?'

'I just found out,' she gasped. 'I just saw the papers. How do I get him out, Charlie. Oh my God, what he's going to do to me!'

'There now, love. Don't cry girl. It's not your fault he lost his temper. There, there now.' Which did serve to mop up some of the tears. 'All you have to do is to go to the court and see the clerk. He'll have a release order for you to sign. When you sign it he'll send one of the bailiffs down to get your boy. You identify him, and you both go free.'

'You mean I—I have to be there with him? I have to stand there—I'd rather be thrown to the lions. He'll kill me right where I stand!'

'Come on, Mary Kate, you're just mouthing words. He can't do any damage, or the judge will cloud up the rain all over him. And let me tell you something else, my dear. The food's terrible in that jail. If I were you I'd bail him out before supper tonight. He'll appreciate that!'

She paced the floor for almost an hour before she

struck on a plan that would get him out and also preserve her neck.

The Principal of the Regional High School made no protest about releasing Becky from class, but the good sister who ruled Mattie's Catholic primary school was fully prepared to do battle. Until Mary blurted out, 'She has to come with me to get her father out of jail!' At which Sister Agatha withdrew from the argument, but later that day made an appointment with the Guidance Director to talk about the type of transfer students being admitted.

So the three of them arrived in New Bedford at two o'clock, in the heavy station wagon. As usual there were no empty parking spaces near the court. Feeling very much abused, she drove the car two blocks farther to the grounds of the Apponoganset Club, and parked ostentatiously in the lot reserved for the exclusive men's club members. 'And it'll serve them right if we contaminate their damn male parking lot,' she muttered as she set the handbrake. 'Come on girls.'

They marched back to the court house three abreast, each of the girls holding one of Mary's arms possessively. They took up more than half the sidewalk, but in this male-dominated area all the looks they got were appreciative. 'They're staring at you, Becky,' Mary teased.

'Come on, Ma,' the girl laughed, 'With your hair in pigtails you look younger than me—I. Whatever.'

'Yes. Whatever.' She tried to laugh, but her throat and mouth were so dry that she could not form the sound. It came out in a choking growl. There were at the foot of the granite steps leading up to the door.

'You all right?' Mattie asked.

'Yes. I'm all right.' She wished desperately for a restaurant where she could get something to moisten her lips. Or a beauty salon where she could hide under a drier for several days. Or perhaps for a huge gryphon who would fly down, pluck them all up, and take them to—Zanzibar?

'Well, if we're going in we'd better get humping,' Becky remarked. 'He's not going to appreciate much more delay!'

'Yes,' Mary returned, 'but—oh hell!'

'He won't eat you, Ma.'

'A lot you know, girl! You'll remember, both of you!'

'Of course,' Mattie responded. 'Stand close to you at all times. Don't let Daddy stand at your side or touch you. Keep between him and you. We got it.'

'Are those reporters by the door waiting for us, Ma?'

'Oh God, I don't know. Don't say a word to them. Just—let's go!'

She climbed the stairs as fast as Mattie's legs would allow. Half a dozen reporters and two photographers blocked the doors. 'Are you going to, Mrs Latimore?' one called. 'Is this an exercise in Women's Liberation?' one of the men asked. 'My paper will pay one hundred dollars for you exclusive story,' a third offered. Two flashbulbs went off in her face, which was gradually turning red. 'Ma's war paint,' Henry used to call it.

She took each of the girls by the hand, lowered her head, and barged into the crowd. One of the cameramen uttered a sharp cry and dropped his camera. 'He wouldn't move,' Becky said, 'so I kicked him in the ankle.' Ahead of them a policeman inside the building noticed their plight. He opened the door and swept a little space free of people. They squeezed into the court house. Mary took two deep breaths and checked the girls out. They both were grinning widely, having enjoyed the encounter.

'Could you tell me how to find——' she started to ask the policeman.

'Second door on the right,' he interrupted. 'He's been waiting for you all morning.'

'The clerk of the court?'

'And your husband too. Better hurry, Ma'am.'

The two girls skipped at her side as they went down the hall. Becky whistled between her teeth. They stopped in front of the door marked six. 'Don't do that, Becky,' she snarled, looking for someone to pick on. 'I've told you before, barking dogs and whistling girls come to no good end!'

'You whistle all the time,' her daughter laughed, 'and look what we've come to. Okay, you've convinced me, I'll stop.'

She wiped her sweaty hand off on her plain navy-blue skirt, palmed the knob, and they went in.

'It's about damn time!' She didn't have to see him sitting in the corner to know he was there. She jumped sideways, pushing the girls in front of her. 'I didn't know,' she whispered. 'I didn't know—until this morning.'

'Then why didn't you come this morning!' he demanded.

'I was—I—I——'

'She was too scared,' Becky interjected. 'How are you, Pop?'

'I'm—well, what do you think,' he said quietly. 'Hi daughters. You both look lovely.'

'So does Ma,' Mattie said.

'Wait until I get these handcuffs off,' he said coldly. For the first time she noticed that his hands were bound in front of him by steel cuffs.

'Over here, Mrs Latimore.' The second voice was high pitched, unruffled. And possessed by an elderly man with a tonsure of white hair, wearing a neat three piece suit. 'You have to sign this form.'

Mary sidled over to the desk, keeping the children between her and her husband. He started to stand up. At the move she jumped back into the corner. 'Make him sit still,' she gasped. the clerk smiled at her, and waved her husband back to his seat. 'Sign here, on all three copies,' he said. Warily she took up the pen, with her eyes glued on Bruce. She felt around to where the clerk's thumb still indicated the lines, and scribbled her name three times.

'That's all that's necessary,' the clerk said. 'You can all go now. If you want to hear the ruling in the case of Latimore versus Somerfield, Judge Osmond intends to open court in about ten minutes.'

'No—no thank you,' she muttered, moving towards the door, 'I just want to——'

'Ah, just a minute, Mrs Latimore,' the clerk called. 'You've forgotten something.'

'Me?' she squeaked.

'No. Him.' The clerk got up from his desk and walked around to Bruce, fishing his pockets for a key to the handcuffs. 'He's released in your custody, Mrs Latimore. You have to take him with you, and you are responsible for his good behaviour, and for his appearance before Judge Osmond on the—ah—twentieth, I believe. There you are, Mr Latimore. If you'll go along with your wife, please.'

'Like a good little boy,' he muttered. He was rubbing his wrists to restore circulation where the cuffs had chafed him.

'Exactly,' the clerk said. There was a little smile playing around his eyes and mouth.

They made a grim foursome as they went out into the corridor. Becky attached herself firmly to Mary's arm, while Mattie grabbed her father's hand. They ploughed through the crowd of reporters, who were still shouting questions. Mary kept her head down and said nothing. Occasionally Bruce said, 'No comment.' They may not have liked his answer, but his very size, his fierceness, his rumpled suit and dirty shirt were enough to shut them off. The four Latimores stalked down the pavement to the car, and got in.

By considerable fast shuffling Becky crowded in to the front seat with Mary, while Mattie steered her father into the back seat. The Devil was sitting behind her, and Mary drove as if she knew it. The air inside the car could have been cut with a knife. Mattie tried to make conversation, but her father was having none of it. Occasionally Mary checked him in the rear-view mirror. He leaned forward in his seat, directly behind her, and glared at the back of her neck. She could not help but shiver. It was bad enough just driving down the road, but when they came to the house, what then? Looking for diversion, her hand snapped on the FM radio, just in time for the local news from New Bedford. As state-wide affairs were discussed, the car turned into Main Street. By the time they had reached the only intersection in town, where Eastboro's one traffic light held sway, the announcer had come to local news. A reporter, evidently still at the court house, described the release from jail. Just as he ended his tale the studio announcer broke in. '*We have just received this flash,*' he said. '*In the case of Latimore Corporation versus Somerfield Farms, Judge Osmond has just ruled that, based on new documentation, the construction company be authorised to proceed. Representatives of the Latimore Corporation announced that construction will begin today.*'

'Well there, little witch,' he snarled from the back seat. 'Justice at last, huh. What do you think of that? Boy, when I get you——'

It was all too much for Mary's torn nerves. She stalled the engine of the car right in the middle of the intersection, and, with horns blaring at her from both directions, she flipped open the car door, and ran. By the time she reached the pavement there was a major traffic jam. A quick look back was enough to show her that he was already involved in an argument with the town's only policewoman. Mary turned and began to trot down Carrerty Street, as fast as she could go.

They're going to build the road! Today! All the scheming, all the planning, all the heartache—and now they were going to build the road, right through the fence, up the side of the hill, through the living room of the farm, and out into the cornfields. They're going to build the road. Right through Becky's home. And I promised the Colonel that I would never let it happen! The tears were streaming silently down her cheeks as she went down the hill by Sullivan Ledge. They're going to build the road. Bruce is going to build the road. Right up the path, over the Liberty Tree! Then they'll pave it eight lanes wide with asphalt, and my heart will be underneath it all. What else was there to do? Only one thing. Personal resistance. Civil disobedience. I'll lie down in front of the first bulldozer. And if Bruce is driving, he'll run right over me! There has to be a better way.

Head down, braids flying, she panted up the hill to the old farmhouse. Her tears had stopped. There was nothing left in her tear ducts, and nothing left where her heart had once beat. Her lips tight, she pushed open the unlocked front door, and went directly to the locked cupboard in the Colonel's study. The key was still in the tobacco box on the mantel. She fished it out, unlocked the gun cabinet, and took out the old double-barrel shotgun. There was no ammunition. The Colonel always stored that in the other end of the house, and she had long since gotten rid of it. 'Damn him!' she muttered as she re-locked the cabinet. 'Damn all men!'

Carrying the shotgun at the ready she went around the perimeter of the house, making sure that the heavy wooden shutters were all closed, and that the back door was closed and bolted. Then she set the lock on the front door, went out on to the little porch, down the three stairs, and waited.

Clouds were billowing up out of the south by four o'clock. Rain clouds, her numbed senses told her. And

then he came. Not with a bulldozer, as she had
expected, followed by a long column of workmen. Just
himself, in the Mercedes. He parked the car down the
track by the Liberty Tree, and started to walk up the
hill towards her.

She stood up and made a big performance of cocking
both barrels of the gun. 'Don't you take another step,'
she called to him. 'You're not going to build a road
through Becky's house, you bastard! Or if you do it'll
be over my dead body!'

He held up both hands, empty, in a sign of surrender.
'Mary Kate,' he yelled, 'We have to talk about this
crazy situation. I don't——' He started to move
towards her again. She watched as his left foot inched
forward. 'I told you to stop!' she yelled back at him.
She raised the gun so that it pointed over his head, and
started to move backwards. The back of her heel came
into contact with the first step on the porch. She
stumbled backwards. Her fingers, on both triggers of
the shotgun, closed in automatic reflex as she fell
backwards, and the gun went off with a roar! The
shotgun jerked backward into her stomach, knocking
her even farther back, spinning her down and around on
the verandah porch so that she was on her hands and
knees, facing out towards him.

'It wasn't loaded,' she whimpered, then louder in a
despairing wail, 'It wasn't loaded!'

He was flat on his face, twenty yards away from her,
doing what any former soldier would do under fire—dig
a hole and crawl into it. It was only then that the
enormity of what she had done came to her. Came to
her because he had lifted his head up off the ground,
and was glaring at her with more malevolence than she
had ever seen. He got up very slowly, brushing the dirt
from his jacket and trousers.

'Mary Kate Latimore,' he growled, 'you've gone too
damn far this time, and you're going to get it, lady, believe

me!' He stomped towards her, looking more like an angry bear than a man. She could actually see the sparks shooting out of his eyes as he face darkened with choler.

With a whimper of fear she ducked back into the house and slammed the door behind her. She was having trouble breathing. She leaned her back against the door, and almost at once it began to rattle as he beat on it from the outside.

'Open this door, Mary Kate,' he bellowed. 'You're only delaying things. Open this damn door!'

She tried to form words, but her lips were trembling, her mouth was dry, and her whole body was shaking. There was a tremendous crash against the door. She slid herself around the wall, and peeked out at him through a break in the shutters. He had found a length of firewood, and was using it as a battering ram against the old lock. And all the time roaring!

She could feel the nausea of fear roiling her stomach, paralysing her will power, grinding her reason into nothing. And then came a double crash—the impact of his battering ram, followed by the ripping sound as the lock was forced, and the door swung heavily back into its floor stop.

She watched him, frozen in position. Snake and mongoose, she thought. Now he really means it. She elevated the shotgun, pointing it straight at his chest. He walked in slowly, imperiously.

'Put—that—gun—down!' he said slowly and softly. She looked from him to it, surprised to see that she was still holding it. Mustering all the strength left in both her hands she pushed the gun away from her, and watched as it fell to the couch in slow motion.

'It wasn't loaded,' she whimpered, almost under her breath. Her hands were stiff and clenched at her sides, her back straight, her chin up, but the tears had started again. Slow, idle drops, easing one at a time out of the corners of each eye.

'That's the only smart thing you've done today,' he snarled at her.

'It wasn't loaded,' she sighed, exhausted. It was hard to keep her head up, hard not to just give up, to collapse at his feet. I'm about to become a statistic, she muttered to herself. Most wives who get murdered are done in by their husbands. 'Well, get it over with,' she sighed at him.

'Oh you needn't worry,' he grated. 'I will. He marched over to her, picked her up, and carried her into the living room. He looked around for a speculative moment, then went over to the hard dining room chair that was kept in the corner for Becky's music lessons. He sat down abruptly and bent her boneless body over his knee.

'No, you can't do that,' she screamed at him. But all her kicking and all her struggling was to no avail. Just one of his hands on her back was enough to lock her into his prison.

'Can't I just do that?' he snarled at her. 'It isn't enough that you make a fool of me for months with your damn legal tricks, and then humiliate me in all the papers by telling them that I don't love you. That's not enough for you, is it. Then you get me locked up in jail and leave me there. And on top of that you have the colossal nerve to shoot at me! Can't do that? Your damn right I *can* do that!'

She gritted her teeth, determined not to give him the satisfaction of hearing her cry. His hand seemed practised. He flipped up her skirts. There was no heat in the house, and the draught struck her before he did. She looked back over her shoulder at his massive hand, raised with palm open, and then ducked her head and bit her lip.

When the hand came down the pain was sharp, the humility worse. She struggled to suppress it, but one small whimper escaped, and the hand came down again. And again. And again.

The last one was too much. She wailed at the pain and the disgrace, and began to shout at him in a gibberish that made no sense. His two hands came to her waist, and he set her up on her feet in front of him, nose to nose. 'Shut up!' he ordered. She was shocked into silence. Her nerves were all numb.

'I'm going to tell you something just one time,' he snarled at her, 'and you damn well better listen. I am going to build this road. And it is going to take the southern alternative route that you proposed. I submitted a request for that change last fall, before Thanksgiving Day. Do you hear me, woman? Before Thanksgiving day. If you and your ten-cent store lawyer had ever looked at the docket you would have known it long ago! Instead, all I've gotten from you is trouble, trouble, trouble. Why didn't you tell me you were studying law? Why did you let me believe it was all Momson's fault? How could you *possibly* have believed that I married you for a lousy mile of road. Why I've got a good notion to——' He gestured towards her with his big right palm again. She shrank away from him. 'Oh, no,' she pleaded. 'No. Please?'

'Well then listen,' he roared at her. 'I married you because I love you. Do you hear me, Mary Kate!'

'I—yes, I hear you,' she stammered.

'And the only thing that keeps us from being happily married, Mary Kate, is that tiny mind of yours. You're so full of suspicion—ah—I ought to whack you some more. You deserved it, didn't you?'

'Y-yes. I deserved it. Yes.'

His hands shifted to her shoulders and he rattled her head around two or three times. 'Now you hear me, Mary Kate,' he snarled. 'I'm going home. You can stay here locked up with your Colonel if you want, or, if you intend to be a good wife to me, you'll come home yourself. And you'd better be there by eight o'clock, you hear?'

She was unable to answer. Her voice was gone, her lips dry, her mind empty, and her nerves were screaming the result of his paddling. Oh how she ached. I love you, he had said. What a fool you've been, Mary Kate Latimore!

His hands dropped away as he stepped back, but he was still peering at her closely with those predatory eyes. Then he put his hands in his pockets. 'Take your choice,' he commanded, and walked out.

She backed up against the sideboard, leaning against it for strength. For the first time in her life she had come to a crisis and had no need to make plans. It was painfully clear to her what she must do. She gulped a couple of deep breaths, and started for the door. The clouds were getting darker, closer. She stumbled painfully down the hill, and over to Henry's house. He was in the kitchen with Anna. They both came out into the hall.

'You look terrible, Ma,' Henry said. 'Sit down here and I'll get you a cup of coffee.'

'No, no,' she quickly replied. 'I—I can't stay. The road is going to be built, Henry, but over the southern bypass. It was all settled in court today.'

'Great news, Ma. We won!' He grabbed her up and swung her around two or three times. The pain struck hard, and tears came to her eyes. 'Please,' she protested. 'Please.' He put her down.

'Are you sure you're all right?' he asked.

'Yes,' she gasped. 'I'm—I'm going back to Bruce to apologise. If he'll let me, I'll be apologising for fifty years.' She turned wearily to the door.

'I'll drive you over,' Henry said. 'It looks like rain.'

'No,' she insisted through clenched teeth. 'You can't do that. I have to walk!'

Henry shrugged his shoulders at Anna. He held the door open for her, and she started out to the road. It had started to rain, a very light sprinkle more associated with spring than with early March. She put her head down and ignored it, concentrating only on where she was putting her feet. Thinking only of what awaited her. 'If you intend to be a good wife,' he had said. Oh Lord, thank you for giving me another chance, she prayed. She reached the county road, and started up the hill at Sullivan's Ledge. The rain came down harder. She paid it no attention. Two cars went by in the other direction. One of them stopped a few feet behind her, made a U-turn, and came up beside her. The passenger door opened. 'Great gobs of monkey grease,' the driver roared at her. 'Get in. What are you trying to do, catch pneumonia?'

'I can't,' she sobbed, and walked by the open door. He slammed his way out of the car, came around, and took her arm. 'Get into the car, Mary Kate,' he said softly.

'I can't!' she returned with all the force she could muster. The rain dripped down her forehead and fell off her nose. She blew out to get it out of her nostrils.

'For God's sake, Mary Kate,' he said more softly, pleadingly. 'I know I've got a terrible temper. I know I should never have hit you. Are you going to hold it against me forever? Get in the car before we both get sick and leave the kids orphans.'

It was the soft tone that did it. She took the two steps that separated them and put her arms up around his neck. 'You should have hit me,' she said, 'and a lot sooner than you did. I love you desperately, Bruce. But I can't get in your car. I can't sit down!' The last part of the sentence came out with a wail.

'Oh Lord,' he said. And then in about two dozen other nicely rounded words that are not in the dictionary, he shouted defiance at the sky, which let loose a revengeful flood of water.

'We're—there's no use both of us drowning, she said into his fourth shirt button. 'Why don't you go on.' By now the rain had penetrated all her clothing. She could feel the drip falling off her skirt on to her shoes. And all the little end-curls had washed out of his hair, leaving it hanging lankly across his forehead.

'Stupid!' he shouted, hitting his forehead with open palm. Mary winced at the sound of it. He snatched open the back door. 'Inside,' he commanded. 'Lie down on your stomach and hold on. Dumb, that's what I am.'

'Me too,' she said sweetly. 'I love you.'

'Well this is a hell of a time to tell me!' It started out as a roar from the front seat, and then became a soft, sweet laugh. 'And I love you too,' he chuckled.

They were home in ten minutes. He helped her up the front stairs and up to the master bedroom, brushing off the laughing enquiries from the children as he went. 'Don't you dare tell them,' she whispered her threat at him as he helped her up the stairs. And then he undressed her, one wretchedly soaked article after another.

'Holy crow,' he muttered, as he unveiled her battered bottom. 'I—I never thought! I hope you'll forgive me, darling?'

'I bruise easily,' she told him as he helped her into the warm shower. 'I can remember once when I was about seven, my mother gave me a whack across my thigh, and her handprint showed for six days. I used to pull up my skirt so everybody at school could see. When she found out, she gave me another one on the other side to "balance the show", she said.'

'It looks awful,' he sighed. 'You stay in the shower for a while, and I'll get something. He was gone for fifteen minutes. When he came back he had a large bottle of ointment and an ice bag with him. He helped her out of the shower, pat-dried her carefully, and stretched her out on her stomach on the bed. The ointment was cold, but she was not about to complain.

It had a soothing, dulling effect, allowing the happiness which had been pinned in a dark corner of her mind for many days to break free. When he added the ice-pack, though, she could not hold back her initial shriek.

'It's only ice,' he said as he slid into the bed beside her. 'I called my doctor in Boston. This is the most hightly recommended emergency treatment. It would happen, just when we get into a position where——'

'Me too,' she agreed. 'It'll be better by tomorrow. I hope.' He had taken off his shirt before he came to bed. She gently shifted herself so that she was partly resting on his chest, pressing one of her breasts into the strength of him.

'I hope so too,' he chuckled. 'This celibate life is for the birds. I haven't had a woman for——'

'Three days,' she interrupted, laughing. 'What a monk you'd make!'

'We've got to plan another holiday,' he said.

'Not right away,' she told him sleepily. The world was catching up to her. 'Parents have responsibilities. We can't go before June. That's when I get my Law Degree, and the kids get out of school.'

'Not so fast,' he murmured in her ear. 'I hadn't made any plans for the kids to come along. November. How about November?'

She lifted slightly to make herself more comfortable. 'Love me, love my kids,' she reminded him. 'November will be a terrible month. I plan to have a baby somewhere along in there.'

His head snapped around, and he looked lovingly down that long arrogant nose at her. 'You mean, Mrs Latimore, that you're pregnant already?'

'No, Mr Latimore,' she sighed, 'Not yet. But we have plenty of time before November, providing we don't waste it. Tell me, what does the P. stand for?'

'What? I don't understand this conversation.'

'In your name. What does the P. stand for?'

'Well,' he chuckled. I don't tell many people that. It stands for Parsifal. My mother was sold on the old German fables when I was born. Parsifal. You know him?'

'Of course I do,' she sighed. 'Do you think I'm uncoutn? Parsifal, the Perfect Knight. The most trustworthy knight in the Empire!'

'Well I'll be damned,' he said. 'What this girl knows!' His left hand had slipped under her shoulders, and her head rested in the middle of his chest, as one of his huge hands toyed with her breast. She levered herself up slightly above him so that she could see his hand cupping her firm, full breast. 'You know what,' she said, 'I like that, but don't touch that little red knob on the top. I think it's my self-destruct button.'

'You can trust me,' he said, and immediately marched his fingers up the mountain to prove that she could not. She jumped as his finger touched her hardened nipple, but the movement stabbed her with pain again.

'Does that hurt,' he asked.

'Only when I laugh,' she retorted dolefully. 'Do you really love me, Mr Latimore?'

'Really love you,' he said. 'Ever since that morning when you met us in the cemetery. Remember that? You were all sparks and fire with me, and all love and devotion with Mattie, and I said right then, that's the girl I want for the rest of my life!'

She squirmed closer, until both her breasts pressed into the curve of his stomach. 'And all I thought of then was that you wanted a mother for Mattie, and a warm body in bed,' she sighed. 'You really sneaked up on me, you devil. The first time I met you I thought you were the most horrible rogue on the face of the earth. I didn't like you at all. And then, after a little while, I didn't not like you. And when we went courting down at the Liberty Tree, I liked you a lot. But do you know when I *loved* you? When Mattie called, and I drove the tractor through the blizzard to Taunton. At first I kept thinking of you, off in warm Arabia, and I yelled at you, and beat on the steering levers, and cursed you as loud as I could yell. And nobody heard. Nobody. So when I got to the bus stop, and found Mattie in that booth, I realised that I loved her, and she said, "And Daddy too?" And before I knew what I was saying, I said, "Yes, and your daddy too!" Tell me, is it true you don't just love me for my body?'

'No, I don't love you just for your body,' he chuckled. One of his hands was tugging at her braids, loosening her hair to fall like a cloud over both of them. 'I love you for your intellect, and for your warmth, and for your compassion, and for your perseverance, and for your bad temper——'

'Bad temper? Me?' she squeaked.

'You,' he continued, '—and for your loyalty, and for your little round red bottom, my dear.'

'Don't you laugh at me,' she said mournfully. 'And you'll promise, of course, that you'll never whack my—whack me again, as long as we both shall live?'

'Don't count on that,' he chuckled. 'Any time you need whacking I'll whack you!'

'Male chauvinist,' she snapped at him sleepily, and nipped the loose skin under his ear with her sharp teeth. 'Tell me so I'll know—when is the next time you're going to whack me?'

'The very next time you point a shotgun at me and tell me that I don't love you,' he said.

'Well, that's all right,' she sighed happily, drowsily. 'I don't think I'll ever make a fool statement like that again, and you don't have a shotgun, do you?'

'No, no I don't,' he said softly. But she was already fast asleep. He slipped his arm out from under her, and went for a cold shower.

Coming Next Month in Harlequin Romances!

2665 PETER'S SISTER Jeanne Allan
A battle-scarred Vietnam veteran shows up in Colorado and triggers painful memories in his buddy's sister. He reminds her of the brother she lost and the love she's never forgotten.

2666 ONCE FOR ALL TIME Betty Neels
When tragedy strikes a London nurse, support comes — not from her fiancé — but from her supervising doctor. But she finds little comfort, knowing he's already involved with another woman.

2667 DARKER FIRE Morgan Patterson
Because she so desperately needs the job, a Denver secretary lies about her marital status. But how can she disguise her feelings when her boss asks her to leave her husband and marry him instead?

2668 CHÂTEAU VILLON Emily Spenser
Her wealthy French grandfather tries to make amends for having disinherited her father. Instead, he alienates Camille and the winery's heir when he forces them to marry before love has a chance to take root.

2669 TORMENTED RHAPSODY Nicola West
The idea of returning to the tiny Scottish village of her childhood tantalizes and torments a young Englishwoman. Inevitably, she'll run into the man who once broke her heart with his indifference.

2670 CATCH A FALLING STAR Rena Young
Everyone in the music business calls her the Ice Maiden. But there's one man in Australia capable of melting her reserve — if only to sign her with his nearly bankrupt recording company.

Introducing
Harlequin Intrigue

INT-3

Because romance can be quite an adventure.

Available in August wherever paperbacks are sold.